Hi Dragana,
   Here's to having
girlfriends like Skylar/
               Annie!

# Bridges

A Daphne White Novel

Enjoy!

8-2-22

D1602954

# Also by Maria Murnane

*Perfect on Paper*
*It's a Waverly Life*
*Honey on Your Mind*
*Chocolate for Two*
*Cassidy Lane*
*Katwalk*
*Wait for the Rain*

# maria murnane

# Bridges

A Daphne White Novel

ISBN-13: 9780980042511
ISBN-10: 0980042518

*To Annie, aka the real Skylar ... for helping me come up with the idea for this book.*

*To Terri, aka Mom #2 ... for encouraging me every step of the way.*

*To Kelly, aka the girl too busy to sleep ... for inspiring Skylar's proclivity for assigning nicknames.*

*And to Blondie, aka Swedish Maria ... for wearing your lovely bracelet to soccer that day!*

# Chapter One

Daphne juggled two sacks of groceries against a hip as she fumbled with her keys, hoping that if she dropped a bag it wouldn't be the one holding the eggs. Once safely inside the house, she rushed into the kitchen, put the eggs, milk, and orange juice into the fridge, then left the nonperishables on the counter before hurrying into her office. She took a seat at the desk and powered on the computer, then checked the time on the screen to see how late she was. Ten minutes. Not that bad for her—but probably ten minutes later than Skylar, whose schedule tended to run like clockwork. She logged into her e-mail account and clicked to open the link Skylar had sent, hoping she wouldn't flub her first-ever attempt at video chatting.

In a flash, her friend appeared on Daphne's computer. "Hi Skylar!"

"Hey hot stuff! It's great to see you, even if it's just on a screen. Can you believe it's been over a year since we were last together in the flesh? Scary how fast time is flying."

"Tell me about it. Emma's junior prom is tomorrow."

"Junior prom? How is that possible? In my head, she's still in diapers. Then again, in my head I still have no wrinkles. Or cellulite."

"I wouldn't mind looking like you," Daphne said.

Seated at her desk in her spacious Manhattan office, Skylar had her auburn locks pulled back into a low ponytail, her lovely face framed by expensive tortoiseshell reading glasses that complemented the tiniest of freckles on her fair cheeks. As always, Daphne thought, her college friend managed to look both appropriately corporate *and* impossibly stylish. She glanced down at her faded jeans and wondered what it would be like to be able to afford nice clothes. She'd been scrimping for so long now that she'd forgotten what it felt like *not* to worry about money.

"Stop it. You look beautiful, as always. So Emma's off to junior prom, eh? Good God, that is horrifying. How old is she now?"

"Sixteen. She's driving. Can you believe it? My little girl behind the wheel?"

"No. I can't believe it. I refuse to believe it, actually."

"Seems like just yesterday she was selling Girl Scout cookies, and at this time next year she'll be getting ready to go off to college." Daphne glanced at a framed photo of her smiling, metal-mouthed daughter on the desk, from back when she wore braces instead of lip gloss. Back before Daphne and Brian split up and Daphne found herself a single mom working part-time at a flower store.

"Does she still want to go to Ohio State?"

"That's the plan, although truth be told it's kind of *my* plan. I don't think I could handle it if she moved far away, so I haven't exactly encouraged her to look at other schools."

"If you want her to come back to Ohio for the long haul, you should encourage her to go to school somewhere she'd never want to live *after* graduation. That's what I'd do if I were in your shoes. A bit of reverse psychology, if you will."

Daphne smiled. "Well, she has really good grades and test scores, so it shouldn't be a problem for her to get into OSU and stay right here in Columbus."

"Sounds like you're not exactly looking forward to the empty nest?"

"Dreading it, to be honest."

Although having the house to herself would give Daphne more time to focus on her writing, which she was thoroughly enjoying. Having put a once-promising career on the back burner to focus on raising her daughter, she'd finally revived a long-abandoned dream harbored by many a young journalism student: to pen a novel. Hers was a work of contemporary fiction loosely based on her own experience as a newly single mother trying to find herself again. After toiling away at her computer for more than a year, she'd recently completed the manuscript, thrilled to have rekindled a passion for storytelling that for years had been buried under the responsibilities of marriage and motherhood.

"What about Northwestern?" Skylar asked.

Daphne blinked, having been lost in thought.

"What about Northwestern what?"

"Is Emma at least going to apply there? I always thought that if I had a daughter it would be cool if she went to Northwestern."

"I don't think so." As she thought of their alma mater, Daphne suddenly remembered the third member of the video call. "Hey, where's KC? Is she on here too and I messed it up? I don't see her."

Her eyes darted around the computer screen. In the backdrop she saw the windows of Skylar's office. Or rather, of Skylar's office when she was working in New York City. Skylar was rarely in one place for long. For years she'd traveled practically nonstop for her job running global sales for a large software company. Daphne didn't know how she found the energy. Then again, Skylar didn't have kids.

"She hasn't logged on yet. I bet she's working out. So what's new on the romance front? Are you still seeing that guy, Derek?"

"Yep, so far so good. We're both really busy though, and of course there's the distance thing." Daphne had met Derek on the joint fortieth birthday trip to Saint Mirika that she and Skylar and KC had taken the year before, but it wasn't until he'd begun coming to Columbus from Chicago for work a few months ago that they'd begun dating.

"Glad to hear it. And your novel? What's going on with that? Has a publisher snatched it up yet?" Skylar had read the first draft and, much to Daphne's delight, had enjoyed it. A lot. Skylar wasn't easy to please, so her stamp of approval meant more to Daphne than she wanted to let on.

"Not yet. I sent it to a bunch of agents a few weeks ago, so I should start hearing back from them soon."

The true number was thirty-six. *Was that too many?* She'd been so excited by the thought of getting published that she'd gone a little overboard with the submissions.

"I bet it's only a matter of time before you'll be swatting the offers away."

"I hope so." Despite the financial stress it had caused, Daphne had loved exercising her storytelling muscles again and was proud of her accomplishment. Getting compensated for it would sure be nice, however. She was definitely looking forward to living less frugally.

"Hey, girls!" KC's tan, smiling face popped up on Daphne's screen. "Sorry I'm so late. I was running a boot camp on the beach and lost track of time."

"Skylar called that," Daphne said with a laugh. KC was in perpetual motion, like a hummingbird. As always, she was dressed in workout clothes, her blonde hair pulled into a ponytail. Her forehead glistened with tiny beads of sweat.

KC touched a finger to her computer monitor. "I've never done a video chat before. This is so cool! It's like you're both right here in my kitchen."

Daphne saw a spice rack and a glass cabinet filled with brightly colored mugs in the background.

"I feel the same way about this thing—like we're in the future," Daphne said.

"Totally! It's so fun to see you both again, even through a computer. Isn't modern technology the best? Hard to believe we didn't have the Internet in college. Can you imagine?" KC said.

"I wouldn't go around broadcasting that fact," Skylar said.

"Why not?" KC asked.

"Because you might as well hang a sign around your neck that says, 'I'm in my forties.'"

"But we *are* in our forties." KC looked confused.

Skylar chuckled. "I'm not disputing that, I'm just saying there's no need to shout it from the rooftop. How's the weather out there in SoCal?"

KC gave a thumbs-up sign. "The usual. Sunny and gorgeous. Max went surfing this morning before work."

"Does he do that every morning?" Daphne asked.

"Not *every* morning. Sometimes he swims, or goes running with me."

Skylar took a sip of coffee. "Athletic people. I will never understand your species."

"You should come out and visit us sometime! Max can give you a surfing lesson."

Skylar coughed. "That will never happen. The surfing lesson, I mean. A trip to visit you and your little beach town is definitely an idea worth discussing, though. So hey, how goes it being the youngest grandma around, or should I say step-grandma?"

"Yeah, how's that going? Are you getting used to it?" Daphne asked.

"It's going pretty great, actually. She's crawling a little, or trying to crawl, I should say. She doesn't get very far before rolling over onto her squishy little back. Max and I can't get enough of her. Hang on a second, I'll show you a photo."

KC stood up and disappeared from the screen, then reappeared with a framed picture of a smiling baby in a light-green onesie that said "I'd rather be at Grandma and Grandpa's."

"Isn't she the cutest?"

"Adorable," Daphne said. "Nice onesie."

"Sounds like someone's gone soft out there," Skylar said.

KC held up a hand. "Guilty as charged. I have to admit, I didn't expect to get such a kick out of being a grandmother, or step-grandmother, or whatever I am."

"You're a superstar, that's what you are," Skylar said. "That little girl could do a lot worse than having a kick-ass grandma like you as a role model. No wonder she looks so happy in that photo."

KC grinned. "Thanks."

Daphne agreed with Skylar.

*How could I not?*

Skylar adjusted her glasses and leaned toward the monitor, her face turning a bit serious. "Anyhow, ladies, thanks for taking the time out of your busy schedules to talk. I hate to cut the chitchat short, but I have a meeting in a few minutes so I don't have much time."

"Is everything okay?" Daphne asked.

Skylar smiled. "Yes, hon, everything's okay. Everything's great, actually. It's just that … well, I have some news."

"Good news, I hope?" Daphne said.

"Yes."

"I love good news!" KC said.

"Are you both sitting down?" Skylar asked. "Because this good news is big news."

"Spill it, already! I'm on the edge of my seat here," Daphne said.

Skylar glanced away from the screen. "Hang on a second." She stood up and disappeared for a moment. It sounded like she closed her office door, then she returned to her desk. "Ladies, I know in a million years you never thought you'd hear me utter the following statement, but ..."

KC leaned forward. "But *what?* The suspense is killing me!"

Skylar paused, then held up her left hand to the screen and yell-whispered, "I'm getting married!"

An enormous diamond ring was perched on her third finger.

KC covered her mouth. "Oh my God!"

Skylar touched a finger to her lips and pointed at her office door. "Careful there, Shouty McShouterson. I think my entire department just heard you. They've probably noticed the ring, but I don't want to make a big deal of it around here."

Daphne was stunned. Skylar had never even been in a serious relationship. And now she was getting married? Daphne didn't even know that Skylar had been seeing anyone.

"That's wonderful news, Skylar. Completely unexpected, but wonderful nonetheless. Who's the lucky guy?"

"His name is James Attingly. He's the CFO of one of my longtime accounts here in Manhattan, but we only met for the first time six months ago. I didn't mention him until now because I wanted to make sure it was the real deal. I hope you understand."

"Of course we understand," KC said. "Don't worry for one second about a silly little thing like that."

*Six months?* Daphne squinted at the screen to get a better look at Skylar.

"Are you pregnant?"

In addition to suggesting many times over the years that she'd probably never choose to get married, Skylar had also pledged not to have children. Those things had just never been in her plan. But her plan had clearly changed. If she was engaged, it wasn't outside the realm of possibility that she was also pregnant.

Skylar laughed. "Definitely not. Can you imagine? I'd be pushing fifty at the kindergarten orientation. No, thank you. I have no desire to be mistaken for a grand-mother. Oops, no offense, KC."

"No offense taken! Your kid *would* be almost the same age as little Julia. Wouldn't that be funny? We could all go on playdates together."

"What a horrifying thought. Trust me ladies, I do not have a bun in the oven. There will be no firearms at my wedding, thank you very much."

"So why get engaged so fast, then? What's the rush?" Daphne asked. "Please don't take that the wrong way. I'm happy for you, just curious."

Skylar shrugged. "I don't know, I guess it just … feels right. I know it's kind of unlike me."

"Coming from someone who patented the rota-tion system of dating, that's *kind of* an understatement," Daphne said.

"Ha ha, true. It's incredibly unlike me. But I don't know, there's just something different about this one. It's like he and I knew each other in a previous life or something. It's hard to explain, but for once I'm all in. So yes, ladies, the rotation system is officially retired."

"I never could figure out how you managed to juggle all those men anyway," KC said.

"It was never more than one at a time, so it wasn't *that* hard. It just was never the same one for long," Skylar said.

"James must really be something special to get you to settle down," Daphne said.

A smile spread across Skylar's face. "He is. He's amazing. He's kind, and smart, and thoughtful, and funny as hell. Sometimes he makes me laugh so hard I can't breathe. You should hear some of his celebrity impressions. *Spot on.*"

"I love him already!" KC yelled.

Skylar pointed in the direction of her office door again. "Jeez Louise! For such a small person, you have a freakishly powerful voice. Can you please keep it down? There are a lot of people who work for me sitting right outside, and I kind of need them to take me seriously."

"How many people?" KC asked.

Skylar furrowed her brow. "In this office? Probably a hundred. Maybe a hundred and fifty."

"Wow." Daphne looked around her tiny home office. "That's a lot more than I have working for me here. Like a hundred and fifty more."

"So you see why I need you to stop yelling, KC? During business hours I like to maintain the facade of professionalism I've worked for two decades to create," Skylar said.

"Sorry, sorry. I'm just so *excited*!" KC managed to whisper a shout this time. "It's just that what you said about James making you laugh reminded me of something. Remember that nice older couple we met on Saint Mirika? They were there to celebrate their fortieth wedding anniversary? Remember what they told us the key to a successful marriage was? *Laughter.*"

Skylar smiled. "I'd forgotten about that until right now."

Daphne hadn't forgotten it. She was still hoping to laugh her way into old age with someone.

KC pressed a finger to her lips, and then against her monitor for a kiss. "*I* didn't forget it. I don't think I'll *ever* forget it, because it's true. So true! And *that's* why I'm so happy for you, Skylar. Over the moon!"

"Thanks, Muppet," Skylar said. "I'm kind of over the moon too."

"I'm happy for you too," Daphne said. "Surprised, but happy."

She couldn't help but reflect on her own romantic situation by contrast. She liked Derek, but there was no way she felt ready to marry him.

"Thanks, hon. I guess it's true when they say 'never say never,' because if anyone thought they'd never get married, it was me. I know that was terrible grammar, by the way," Skylar said.

Daphne smiled. "I think you get a pass on grammar today."

"Have you set a date?" KC asked.

"No date yet, but that brings me to the reason for this call."

"Are you saying you have *more* news?" KC asked.

"I don't think I can take any more news. I'm still trying to process the original news," Daphne said.

"No news, just an invitation. I'd like to invite my two oldest and dearest friends to New York for a girls' weekend to celebrate. And to help me find a dress. And to drink a lot of wine. What do you think?"

"You mean a bachelorette party?" KC said.

Skylar waved a hand in front of her face. "Please. I'm in my fifth decade. I refuse to call it a *bachelorette party*. Let's call it a girls' weekend."

"So no white sash and tiara for you, then?" Daphne asked with a fake frown.

Skylar cringed. "Oh God, can you imagine? I'm so glad cell phone cameras weren't around to capture the days when we used to do that sort of thing. I don't want any evidence floating around that I ever took part in such drunken debauchery. Not that I'm *against* drunken debauchery—now I just prefer a more dignified version of it."

KC raised her hand. "Well, whatever you want to call it, I'm in. I love drunken debauchery, dignified or otherwise."

"That's because you're so healthy it takes you like one cocktail to get drunk," Skylar said.

"That is a good point," KC said.

"When did you have in mind for this little nonbachelorette weekend?" Daphne asked.

"Would Fourth of July weekend work?" Skylar said.

KC raised her hand again. "In!"

"You don't want to check with your husband first?" Skylar asked.

KC shook her head. "Not necessary. Max knows that when it comes to getting the Three Musketeers together, I have a *never say no* policy. It's written in pen on the back of our marriage license."

Skylar whistled. "Oooh, I like that. I might have to do that with my own marriage license. What about you, Daphne?"

"Hang on, I have my calendar right here. Daphne flipped ahead several weeks to the date in question, then nodded. "Looks good to me. Emma's with Brian that weekend."

Skylar snapped her fingers. "Perfect! Then let's book it. I'm paying for your flights, by the way."

"You don't have to do that," Daphne said. Managing the cost of a ticket on her tight budget had already crossed her mind, however. Flying to New York on a holiday weekend had to be expensive, especially on relatively short notice.

"I insist, so don't even try to argue with me about it. I'll book the flights and e-mail you both the details. You can stay with me, unless you'd rather stay in a hotel? No, scratch that. I *insist* you stay with me. It will be so much more fun that way, like an extended slumber party. James has a golf trip planned that weekend, so I can focus entirely on you two."

KC stood up from her kitchen stool and did a little celebratory dance. "This will be so fun! I've never been to New York. Can we go for a run in Central Park?"

"*You* can go for a run in Central Park. Be careful throwing around those pronouns." Skylar looked at Daphne. "Did I get that right? *We* is a pronoun, yes?"

"*We* is indeed a pronoun. Well done. I'll go running with you, KC. Being around you always motivates me to get in better shape."

"That's the spirit! I love motivating people!" KC pumped a fist.

"You can try motivating me all you want, but while you two go off and sweat to death in the heat, I will happily remain inside with my air-conditioning, thank you very much. I'll be traveling practically nonstop until then and will probably just want to park my rear end on the couch for a few days and chill," Skylar said.

"I'm not good at lying on the couch," KC said. "I get antsy."

"I guess we all have our own ways of relieving stress," Daphne said.

"My thoughts exactly," Skylar said. "Your workout is my blowout."

Daphne laughed. "I'm not sure what that means, but you do have really nice hair."

"Do you have room for both of us at your place?" KC asked. "I've always heard New York apartments are like shoe boxes."

Skylar held up a palm. "We've got room, no worries."

"We?" Daphne said.

"James and I, hon."

"You're *living* together?" Daphne asked.

"Officially shacking up as of a month ago," Skylar said. Then she glanced at her watch. "Okay, lovelies, I've got to skedaddle to a meeting. Can't wait to see you both and catch up on all the happenings." She blew them a kiss and disappeared from the screen.

"Bye Daphne!" KC waved, and then she too evaporated.

Daphne logged off as well, then reached for a pad of sticky notes and jotted down a reminder to request time off from the flower store over Fourth of July weekend. She hoped to have some good news of her own to celebrate by then. She looked across the room at a bookcase. It was lined with her favorite stories, the ones she'd read over and over throughout the years. She pictured her own name among the spines in the not-too-distant future. A tiny smile crept across her lips as she thought about how incredible that would feel.

She taped the sticky note to her monitor and decided to go for a run after putting away the rest of the groceries. As she laced up her shoes and headed out the door into the crisp afternoon, she felt a happy flutter of anticipation at the thought of spending a weekend with her best friends— and in New York City! Back in college, she'd considered moving there after graduation, visualizing herself as an intrepid young reporter riding the subway each day en route to a job at the *New York Times*. But that was a lifetime ago, and things had turned out differently than she'd once imagined. Jogging past the picture-perfect houses and tidy lawns of suburbia, she wondered what her life would be like now had she chosen that path. She'd never know, but at least she was writing again—and delighted about it.

# Chapter Two

"Well hello there, neighbor. You're looking very sporty this afternoon."

"Hi Carol," Daphne slowed her pace to a walk and put her hands on her hips to catch her breath, having just finished a three-mile loop through the tranquil streets of Grandview.

"Is Emma all ready for her dance tomorrow? She's really growing up, that one." Carol and her husband, whose own kids were grown and had children of their own, had lived across the street since the day Daphne and Brian moved in as newlyweds nearly twenty years ago.

"Tell me about it. I just had a video call with my college friends. Seems like not that long ago *we* were Emma's age. Then again, it also seems like a lifetime ago. Funny how that is."

"So you had a chat with the other two Musketeers? How are they doing?"

"You remember that we call ourselves the Three Musketeers?"

"Of course I do. You don't talk about them much, but it's hard not to see that you have a little glow about you when you do. I can see it right now, in fact."

"They're good. Better than good, actually. Skylar's getting married—that's what the call was about. She invited us to New York for a girls' weekend to celebrate, although I fear we might be a little old to call it a *girls'* weekend. Skylar won't even call it a bachelorette party, for the same reason."

Carol clasped her hands together. "Nonsense! You're never too old for a girls' weekend *or* a bachelorette party. You'll have a glorious time. Norman and I just love New York. It's been a few years since we've been there, but it seems like one of those magical places that just never changes. Have you ever been?"

"No, so I'm already counting the days. I always have so much fun with those two no matter where we are, but New York sure makes for a pretty appealing setting. Plus I hope to have heard back about my novel by then too, which could give us something else to celebrate. Wouldn't *that* be perfect timing?"

"That's right! Your novel! So you sent it off to publishers then, did you?"

"Not exactly. I sent it to agents. They're the ones who connect you with the publishers, kind of like the way agents get actors their roles in movies and on TV."

"Ah, got it. Well, it all sounds so exciting! I wish you the best of luck, my dear. You've certainly worked hard enough on that manuscript, and God knows you deserve a little sunshine in your life. I promise to be first in line at your book signing. I've already told all the ladies in my book club that *my neighbor* is going to be a published author. They're all quite impressed." She beamed with pride.

"Thanks Carol. That's very sweet of you."

Carol had been there for Daphne throughout her divorce and had never once wavered in her conviction that Daphne would get through it. Daphne hadn't believed that for a long time, but in the end Carol had been right. Daphne had finally emerged from the darkness, feeling almost like her old self again. She knew she'd never be exactly the same, but no one stayed exactly the same forever—even people whose dreams of happily ever after *didn't* turn to dust. When she'd first toyed with the idea of writing a novel about a divorced woman in her late thirties, Carol had insisted that she get to work. Her unwavering support had helped Daphne stay focused, especially when she'd been tempted to give up early on. But eventually things started to click and Daphne found her storytelling mojo again. She also found engaging in the creative process both cathartic and invigorating. It just felt ... *right*.

Carol nodded in the direction of her front door. "Well, my love, I've got to get inside to start dinner. Give Emma a kiss for me, will you?"

"Will do. Bye Carol."

Once inside her house, Daphne picked up the phone to call Derek.

"A call from a beautiful woman in the middle of the afternoon? To what do I owe this pleasant surprise?" he said.

"Guess who's spending Fourth of July weekend in New York City?"

"The Big Apple? Did you get a job on Broadway?"

"If you heard me sing, you wouldn't be asking that. You weren't planning to be here that weekend, were you?"

"Not anymore, I'm not."

"Oh no! Did I just mess up?"

"Kidding. I have the boys that weekend."

"Phew. I must say, dating a divorced man has its benefits."

"You mean because I too bow to the power of the all-mighty custody calendar?"

"Bingo."

"So what's happening in New York?"

"Skylar invited me and KC to come for a visit. She just got … engaged." Daphne flinched, immediately regretting having told him that. Revealing how quickly Skylar had gotten engaged might inadvertently put pressure for things between them to develop faster than they were, and she was determined to take the relationship slowly so as not to make another mistake—although Derek had also been burned by divorce and didn't seem to share her hesitation.

Just then, Daphne heard the mumbled sound of a man saying something to Derek, then Derek's voice again. "Got it, be right there. Sorry Daphne, I have to run to a meeting. Call you later, okay?"

•  •  •

That night, Daphne was still trying to wrap her head around Skylar's news. Daphne was finally getting used to the idea of dating after having spent most of her adult life with Brian. Skylar, who had spent most—no *all*—of her adult life dating, was getting married? It was as if their lives had somehow flip-flopped.

*Now* that *would make for a good book.*

Her thoughts then turned to the manuscript she'd worked on tirelessly for so many months, and she felt a shiver of anticipation at how her life might soon change.

*A published author!*

She imagined all the promotional activities that would entail, things up to now she'd seen only in movies. Press interviews, meet-and-greets, writers' conferences, speaking engagements, book-club appearances, signings with fans.

*Actual fans!*

It would be a dream come true, albeit one she'd put off pursuing for years so Brian could focus on his career. But all the fun marketing stuff would be the icing on the cake. For *her*, the cake was simply sitting at her desk and writing. With Emma's high school graduation looming in the not-too-distant future, a new focus was just what Daphne needed. A budding writing career to pour her energies into would make Emma's leaving home feel less like an ending and more like a beginning. And who better to celebrate that beginning with than her two best friends?

She couldn't wait for Fourth of July weekend to arrive.

# Chapter Three

In what seemed like a blink to Daphne, it was the Friday of Fourth of July weekend. Emma had left the night before to spend the long weekend backpacking with Brian and his wife, so after Daphne finished packing she laced up her running shoes for a quick workout before leaving for the airport.

She hoped the exercise would cheer her up, but she was wrong. As she completed her usual loop through her neighborhood, she felt sluggish. And depressed. Though she *should* have been in the best of spirits—she was about to get on a plane to go meet her best friends, after all—she was disheartened by the feedback she'd been getting from literary agents. She'd been so eager to arrive in New York with life-changing news—ready to celebrate and officially kick off her new career as an author—but, contrary to Skylar's prediction that Daphne would be swatting them away likes flies, every agent to respond so far had turned her manuscript down.

The rejections she'd received were polite but clearly boilerplate messages of various phrasings, and they all said essentially the same thing: no. She'd gotten a handful of *I enjoyed it, but unfortunately it's just not for me,* a few *I wish I could say yes but I just can't,* and several *You deserve an agent who is passionate about your project* or a variation thereof. Almost every agent said she had talent, which had been a maddening kind of compliment.

*If I have talent, why won't they help me develop it? Why would they say I have talent if they didn't believe it?*

And with no specific feedback from them on the manuscript itself, she wasn't sure *why* they were turning it down, so her mind began a tortuous loop of questions to which she had no answer.

*Is my writing awful? Is the story boring? Is it a combination? Did I write a boring story badly?*

She'd been an honors student in the esteemed journalism school at Northwestern.

*That had to mean something, right?*

Granted, that was two decades ago, but at this point she was willing to grab on to anything that would keep her from spiraling down the rabbit hole of self-doubt.

Just a few weeks earlier, she'd thought the timing of the weekend would be fortuitous—that her imminent success would be part of the celebration. But now she thought the opposite. With each literary agent she checked off her list, that joyful anticipation of seeing her friends had dissipated—and a feeling of dread had seeped in to replace it. Loathe as she was to admit it, if the few remaining names on her list were going to follow suit and reject her, the last person she wanted to be with when that happened was Skylar, who *radiated* an aura of success.

Back when they'd both finished college near the top of their class, Daphne had been full of the same confident ambition as Skylar, eager to turn her love of language and storytelling into a career, energized by the idea of having *her words* appear on the page for strangers to read—and enjoy. For a brief period after graduation, she'd been a rising star at a magazine and even won a couple of writing awards, but then she'd fallen in love and one thing had led to another. And now Skylar was a wildly successful executive. And Daphne was decidedly not.

● ● ●

Showered, packed, and ready to go, Daphne sat down at her desk to check her e-mail one last time before leaving for the airport.

*Maybe today is the day I'll finally get the news I want? All it will take is one yes, right?*

She projected all the positive energy she could summon onto the screen as she logged into her account.

She had one new message, from Wilson Literary.

She leaned forward and held her breath as she clicked to open it.

*This is going to be the one, I know it!*

*Dear Daphne, thanks for submitting your manuscript. While I enjoyed the story and think you have talent, I just don't think it's right for my list, so I cannot offer*

*you representation at this time. I wish I could say yes, but this is a tough industry and you deserve an agent who is truly passionate about your project.*
*I wish you the best of luck.—AW*

Daphne fell back against her chair, the wind out of her sails. She read the e-mail again and sighed. AW of Wilson Literary had used three stock rebuffs in her rejection. It was as if she were yelling "no" three times in a row.

*NO! NO! NO! You are NOT a good writer! WHO CARES how good you were twenty years ago?*

Daphne quietly stood up and turned off her computer, trying not to cry. She'd now heard back from all but three of the agents she'd contacted. Thirty-three of thirty-six on her list had turned her town.

*Thirty-three of thirty-six.*

She made her way back to the foyer and reached for her purse and suitcase, smiling wistfully as she locked the front door behind her. For perhaps the first time in her life, she was glad that math wasn't her strong suit, as she didn't want to know what thirty-three out of thirty-six translated into, percentage-wise.

• • •

While in line at the airport ticket counter, Daphne's phone rang. She glanced at the caller ID and hesitated for a just a moment before answering.

"Hi. I'm just about to check in and may have to hang up on you, so consider yourself warned," she said.

"Warning considered," Derek said. "Excited for the big bachelorette weekend?"

Daphne smiled. "I told you, Skylar has been very clear that it's not called a bachelorette weekend when you're in your forties."

"So no male strip clubs, then?"

"I'm pretty sure that's not on the agenda, thank God."

"What *is* on the agenda?"

"I have no idea, actually. When I'm with Skylar, she runs the show. I'm happy just to go along for the ride."

She was tempted to share her disappointment about the mounting rejections of her manuscript but decided not to bring it up. Right now, she just wanted to forget about it and try to have fun with her friends. No, she *would* have fun with her friends. She was determined to stay positive. She forced a smile into the phone.

"What about you? What do you have planned for the weekend?"

"A lot of soccer-dad stuff, although no actual soccer will be involved. I think we have a baseball tournament, a swim meet, and two birthday parties. The usual chaos."

"So you have the boys all weekend?"

"Tonight through most of Sunday. I'm dropping them off at Barbara's after the second birthday party on Sunday afternoon. Or maybe it's the third birthday party. I need to consult the activity calendar on my refrigerator. That thing's a monster."

"As you know, I have one of those on my fridge too. Packed to the gills for just one kid, so I can only imagine what it's like for two. Any big plans for the Fourth itself?"

Silence.

"Derek?" Daphne said.

"Sorry about that. A coworker just popped his head into my office."

"No problem."

"So hey, I've been meaning to ask you something. How would you feel about spending the weekend after next at my buddy's lake house in Michigan? He said we could use it."

Daphne felt a lump form in her throat. She'd never traveled to visit Derek.

When she didn't respond right away, Derek spoke again. "You still there? Did I just scare you away?"

"No, of course not." She swallowed. "When do you need to know?"

*Derek's smart and kind and really seems to care about me, so what am I so afraid of? It's a weekend at a lake house. It's not as if he's proposing marriage.*

"Could you let me know by Monday? I think we'd have a great time, but no pressure."

"Let me check my schedule, okay?" Daphne glanced at all the couples in line, at all the families getting ready to go on vacation together, and decided to table the discussion for the moment. "I've really got to run now, I'm sorry. I'll call you from New York, okay?"

"Okay, sure. Safe travels, Daphne."

"Bye." Feeling a twinge of guilt for cutting the call short when she didn't *really* need to, she hung up wondering if anyone around her had overheard her conversation, and if it was super obvious that she was being wishy-washy. She knew she should be excited by the idea of spending a weekend away with Derek, but for some reason she wasn't.

*Maybe I'm just not ready to date again? Maybe* that's *the problem?*

When she reached the front of the line a few minutes later, Daphne handed her driver's license to the ticketing agent. Because Skylar had made the reservation, Daphne hadn't paid attention to anything but the departure time and flight number. As the agent tapped away at his keyboard, she quietly waited, hoping she didn't have a middle seat. Then the agent smiled and gave her a boarding pass. Daphne thanked him and checked for her seat assignment as she began walking away, then did a double take and froze.

She turned back to the counter. "I'm in seat 2A?"

"Yes, ma'am."

"Is that in first class?"

He looked amused. "Yes, ma'am. Enjoy your flight."

# Chapter Four

Several hours later, Daphne stepped out of a cab in front of a modern apartment building located in the Tribeca neighborhood of Manhattan. She wheeled her suitcase into the lobby and approached the doorman—*Or is he a concierge?*—standing behind a tall desk flanked by two potted plants in black ceramic pots. The area was small but sleek.

"May I help you?" he asked with a friendly smile.

"Hi, um … yes. My name's Daphne White, I'm a friend of Skylar Flanagan's." She suddenly realized that she didn't know Skylar's apartment number.

*Did Skylar even give it to me?*

"Ah, yes. Ms. Flanagan is expecting you. Do you need help with your luggage?"

"I'm fine, thanks. Which unit is she in?"

The doorman gestured to the elevator. "Take the elevator to the ninth floor."

"Which apartment number?"

"Just the ninth floor."

Daphne knitted her brow. "I'm sorry?"

"It's the entire ninth floor."

Daphne felt her cheeks flush. "Oh. Thank you."

*The entire ninth floor? What does that mean?*

The doorman smiled and bowed his head. "Enjoy your stay."

Feeling way out of her league, Daphne wheeled her suitcase into the elevator. She watched the number tick up and wondered what Skylar's apartment would look like. A few moments later, the door quietly opened to what resembled a mezzanine of a hotel, not a single-family dwelling. Daphne stepped forward and swiveled her head to take in her surroundings. To her left was a wide staircase—one flight of steps went downward—and another upward.

*How big* is *this place?*

To her right was an entryway to a kitchen, the door half-open. Beyond the staircase was what appeared to be a fully stocked bar, complete with barstools and glass cabinets filled with stemware. She took a few tentative steps forward on the hardwood floors and saw that across from the bar to the right was a spacious living room with a large sectional couch and ottoman atop a plush, cream-colored area rug. The largest flat-screen TV she'd ever seen was mounted to the wall. Beyond the floor-to-ceiling windows, the skyscrapers of the Financial District gleamed in the distance. Aside from the few pieces of furniture and the TV, the room was minimally decorated.

Daphne blinked. *Skylar lives* here?

Returning to the elevator, she dropped her suitcase and poked her head into the kitchen to steal a peek—and was again dumbstruck by the vast size and opulence of what she saw. A sparkling oval ring of copper pots and pans hung above a large marble island, flanked by custom shelving, a farmhouse sink, and a Sub-Zero refrigerator. Daphne had always dreamed of having a large, beautiful kitchen with a marble island, but this was beyond anything she'd ever imagined. Way beyond. She quietly walked back to the elevator and stood there, not sure whether to stay put or send out a search party for her friend in the cavernous apartment.

"Hello?" she called out. "Skylar?"

"Daphne? Is that you, sweets?" Skylar's voice boomed from somewhere.

Daphne thought it came from down below but couldn't be sure. She stepped toward the stairwell and looked up, then down.

"Skylar? Where are you?"

"Hang on! I'll be right up!" She was apparently downstairs.

Just then Daphne heard a beeping sound, signifying that she had a new e-mail. She pulled her phone out of her purse and braced herself when she saw an agent's name.

*Maybe* this *is the one? The timing would certainly be good.*

Hoping the tides would finally turn in her favor, she again willed herself to direct positive energy at the device, as if that could somehow alter the contents of the message by sheer force of determination. She clicked to open it, her heartbeat speeding up with anticipation.

She eagerly began to read, then immediately felt deflated as she was met with yet another *I wish you the best of luck finding more suitable representation,* perhaps the most popular of all the boilerplate rejections she'd seen.

*Have I failed as a novelist before I've even begun?*

She knew it was tough out there, but she had no idea it was *this* bad. Given the emotional hurdles she'd jumped over just to get herself to *write* a book, not to mention the financial sacrifices it required, it had never occurred to her that the story might not make it off the pages of her laptop. She slipped her phone back into her purse and told herself to stay optimistic. She still had two agents to hear from.

*Two's better than none, right? And all it will take is one yes. Maybe I will beat the odds.*

A moment later, Skylar trotted up the stairs, dressed in a black sleeveless top and loose white pants, her shiny auburn locks hanging a few inches below her shoulders, the spectacular diamond gleaming on her left ring finger. "There you are!" She embraced Daphne in a warm hug. "How was your flight? That was my bad for having Stephen send you up here. I should have told him to send you to the eighth floor."

Daphne hugged her back. "The flight was fine. How many floors *is* this place?"

"Three. Four, if you count the roof deck."

Daphne's eyes widened.

"I know, it's a little over the top. James loves it though, so what can you do?"

"Oh, so *he* owns it?" Daphne secretly hoped that was the case because that would make her feel less, well, poor. She knew perfectly well that she wasn't *actually* poor, but just then she felt like a frumpy country bumpkin. She didn't want to compare her financial situation to Skylar's—that would be like comparing grapes to cantaloupes—but an apartment like this made it hard not to do so.

Skylar shook her head. "We bought it together, just moved in last month. I think I may have mentioned that when we talked? I can't remember—it's all been such a blur."

"I can imagine. Hey, speaking of James, tell me all about him! What's he like? Will we get to meet the man who finally got you to settle down?"

"He left today for a golfing weekend, so unfortunately not this time. You'll like him though, everyone does. He's very smart but a little goofy—he does a Jack Nicholson impression that has me on the *floor*—so when people first meet him socially they often underestimate what's going on inside that salt-and-pepper head of his. Professionally though he's like I am, kind of a hard-ass, so we're a good match that way. We always laugh about putting our work personalities on every morning along with our suits."

"Wow! He does sound like a perfect match for you. That's fantastic, Skylar. Do you have a picture?"

"I have one downstairs and a bunch on my phone, but nothing up here. I know, I'm terrible. This place is so barren that I don't even have a framed photo of myself and my fiancé in our living room! I really need to start decorating but haven't had a free second. I'm still getting used to not having my own place, but I guess when you marry someone you should probably live with him." She chuckled and put her hands on her hips. "I'm just glad we have enough space so we're not on top of each other all the time. After so many years living by myself, I need to be alone once in a while, you know? I love me a little Skylar time."

Daphne eyed her surroundings again. "I suspect making room for a little Skylar time is *not* a problem here. Did you guys rob a bank or something? This is a mansion!"

Skylar laughed. "It *is* a little extravagant for my taste, that's for sure, but I'm getting used to it. I'll give you the grand tour when KC gets here. How about a glass of wine while we wait? Kick up our feet and relax a bit?"

"Sounds like a perfect plan." Daphne started toward the bar, but Skylar caught her arm.

"Actually, I was thinking we'd go up on the roof deck. There's a bar up there too, and it's so nice outside. Let's take advantage of the weather."

"There's a bar on the roof deck? How does that work?"

"What do you mean?"

"I mean with the other people who live in the building. How do you stock it?"

"Oh no, hon, we don't have to share it with anyone. The roof deck is part of the apartment. The *best* part, in my opinion."

Daphne snapped her fingers. "Got it. *Actually*, now that I think of it, the roof of my house has a private bar too. It's solid gold. And embedded with diamonds."

Skylar laughed. "It's so good to see you. Now let's go have ourselves a drink and catch up, shall we?"

"You don't have to ask me twice." Daphne turned on her heel toward the elevator, but Skylar again put a hand on her arm, this time nodding toward the kitchen area. "There's a separate elevator for the roof deck."

"A *separate* elevator?"

Skylar interlaced her arm with Daphne's. "Makes it easier to entertain. This way."

As the two of them made their way toward the second elevator, Daphne tightened her grip on her weathered purse and stole a peek at her sandals, wishing they weren't quite so scuffed. Oh how she hoped for good news from an agent—just *one* agent—and soon.

# Chapter Five

Daphne and Skylar had just taken their seats in all-weather wicker lounge chairs on the roof deck when the elevator door opened. Daphne turned her head expecting to see KC, but out hopped a woman she didn't recognize. Short and brunette, she looked to be several years younger than Skylar.

"I have arrived," the woman said as she curtsied. "Let the games commence."

"Hey, Krissa!" Skylar stood up and hugged her, then turned to Daphne. "Daphne, this is Krissa, my best gal pal here in New York. Krissa, this is Daphne, one of my two best gal pals from college."

Krissa held out a hand as Daphne stood up too. "It's nice to meet one of the Three Musketeers in person. Skylar's been singing your praises, and you know how particular she is, so I've been looking forward to this."

"I hate to think what she's said—this is a woman who's seen me sporting bangs bigger than that fern over there," Daphne said as she shook Krissa's hand.

"For the record, my bangs were as big as Daphne's if not bigger, so I'm hardly one to cast judgment. But now to the business at hand." Skylar gestured to the bar.

"What can I get you to drink? We're enjoying a lovely chardonnay, but I can make you whatever you want."

"Chardonnay sounds great to me. I dig a cold glass of white wine on a warm evening."

Daphne lifted her glass. "Excellent choice."

"You got it, honey. Hang on." Skylar ducked behind the bar and poured Krissa a glass, then the three of them settled into the lounge chairs.

"Is this your first time in New York?" Krissa asked Daphne.

"Yes. Back in high school I applied to Columbia, but I never came to visit the campus. I guess I chickened out because I was intimidated by the idea of living in such a big city."

"I was like that too when I first got here, kind of wide-eyed. But before I knew it I was walking really fast and cursing under my breath at slowpoke tourists along with everyone else," Krissa said.

"God, those people drive me nuts," Skylar said. "I know I shouldn't judge, but why do they have to walk so slowly?"

"So that was that?" Krissa said to Daphne. "You never came?"

"That was that. And while a part of me still wonders what it would have been like to go to school here, once I visited Northwestern I knew that's where I wanted to be. I think it was a better fit for me, at least at that stage of my life."

"*I'm* sure glad you made that decision, or else we never would have met," Skylar said.

"I think it's great that you're still so close after all these years. I don't really keep in touch with many people from Penn State," Krissa said.

"Yep, still thick as thieves," Skylar said. "And it was more than just friendship that I got back then from this one. Daphne was such a good student she pushed me to work harder than I wanted to all through college, but I'm so glad she did. I made the dean's list every semester because of her."

"Please, *you* were the smart one," Daphne said.

*And the successful one.*

She turned her head to take in the view of the Wall Street skyline, and a wave of insecurity rolled over her.

"Call me crazy, but if you were both making regular appearances on the dean's list at Northwestern, I think it's safe to say that you're *both* pretty smart," Krissa said.

"I guess we both have our strengths. Daphne's always been a gifted writer. In fact, she just wrote a book."

Krissa cocked an eyebrow. "Really? Now *that's* impressive. What kind of book? Fiction? Nonfiction?"

"A novel," Daphne said.

"What genre?"

"I guess you'd call it contemporary fiction? I'm not exactly sure." She knew it was thinly veiled reality, granted, but fiction nonetheless.

"What's it about?" Krissa asked.

Daphne took a sip of her wine, dreading where the conversation was going. "It's … uh, it's about a divorced woman who reunites with her college friends on a tropical island to celebrate turning forty."

"Sounds fun," Krissa said.

"It is. I read it," Skylar said. "Of course I'm biased because one of the characters is based on me, but I thought it was really good. It made me laugh *and* cry."

"A character is based on you? So is the story based on a real trip?" Krissa said.

Daphne swallowed. "I guess so, loosely."

"Not *that* loosely," Skylar said. "Especially the part about the main character meeting an attractive younger man—while walking on the beach no less—and having her first post-divorce fling. That scene was just *made* for a book."

"You had a holiday fling with a hot younger man? I love that! How hot and how much younger?" Krissa asked.

"Very hot," Skylar said.

Daphne pursed her lips. "In the book, he's about ten years younger. In real life I'm not exactly sure. Maybe eleven, twelve years? He said he was getting close to thirty, but I never came right out and asked for an exact number."

"Nice! That's just what age is, a *number*, so good for you. And good for your main character too. What's her name?"

"Lexi," Daphne said.

Krissa nodded. "Good for Lexi. That sort of stuff is empowering for female readers. I hate the way our society practically celebrates older men who date younger women while criticizing older women who date younger men. What's up with that? I think it's stupid."

Skylar lifted her glass toward Krissa. "I couldn't agree with you more. It's a total double standard. Regardless of age, that guy was *lucky* to be with Daphne, and he damn well knew it."

Daphne gave Skylar a grateful look, and Skylar winked in acknowledgment before continuing. "He was a hunk in real life too. What was my nickname for him, Daphne? Hottie McHotness? Hunkie McHunkerson?"

"His name was Clay *Hanson*, but you called him Clay *Handsome*."

"Ah, yes. That was a good one," Skylar said with a chuckle. "I do like my nicknames."

"I like everything about this conversation," Krissa said. "What's his name in the book?"

"Cole Harrington," Daphne said.

"Oooh, I like that. I can already picture him in swim trunks—or better yet, *out* of swim trunks." Krissa turned to Skylar and held up her wine glass. "Hey, can you top me off before I finish this deliciously refreshing beverage? That way it only counts as one drink before dinner, which makes me less of a lush, at least on paper."

Skylar stood up and patted Krissa on the head. "You got it, sweets."

"So are there steamy sex scenes with this guy in the book?" Krissa asked Daphne.

Daphne blushed. "Not really. It's more of a fade-to-black image, you know, to let the reader's imagination fill in the blanks? It's not really my style to write that sort of thing. I get too embarrassed."

"I can understand that. I don't know if I could write the hot-and-heavy stuff either. Not that I have any problem *reading* it, mind you," Krissa said. "That's the beauty of the Kindle. No one knows if you're reading Shakespeare or smut."

Skylar refilled Krissa's glass and resumed her seat. "I'm in the same boat. I think anytime I'd begin to type a sex scene I'd imagine my prim Irish mother reading it, and *boom!* a figurative bucket of ice water would be thrown all over the screen."

Daphne laughed. "Sounds about right."

"So back to real life. You *really* met this guy on the beach?" Krissa asked Daphne.

"Yep. I was taking a walk the first day we got to the island, and he and a bunch of his friends were staying in a house near ours. He kind of called out to get my attention from the deck, and we started chatting. For some reason he was out there all by himself. I can't remember why."

"His buddies were probably all hungover and napping," Skylar said.

"Let me guess—they were there for a bachelor party?" Krissa said.

Daphne looked surprised. "How did you know?"

"Guys around the age of thirty usually take beach vacations for one of only two reasons, and that's either they or one of their buddies is getting married, or they're with a companion of the female persuasion."

"I never thought about that before, but it makes sense. I bet you're right," Daphne said.

"I'd put *money* on a bet that she's right," Skylar said. "If anyone knows the habits of single men, it's Krissa."

"I've become somewhat of an expert on the subject, that is true. It's not something I'm particularly proud of, but hey, what can you do?" Krissa took a sip of her wine. "I'm a product of my environment, much like a perfectly smooth stone on the shore of a beach. So did you ever talk to the guy after you got back from the trip?"

Daphne shook her head. "He gave me his number, but I think he was probably just being nice, so I dropped it."

"You don't *know* that he was just being nice. In my experience, men don't give their numbers to women they don't want to hear from. Hey—wait a minute. Didn't he live here in New York?" Skylar asked.

"Yes. At least he did a year ago. I have no idea if he's still here."

Krissa's eyes got big. "He lives *here*? No way. Are you going to text him?"

"I don't think so," Daphne said.

"Why the hell not?" Krissa said.

"She's dating someone now," Skylar said.

"Ah, got it," Krissa said. "Lucky you."

Daphne bit her lip. "Regardless, I think it's probably better to let Saint Mirika stay in the past."

# Chapter Six

"How's the Ice Princess doing?" Krissa asked Skylar.

Skylar sighed and leaned back into her chaise lounge. "The same. Frosty, cold, chilly. Any and all of those adjectives still apply."

"Who's the Ice Princess?" Daphne asked as she returned from the far end of the roof deck, where she'd been admiring the scenery. The view comprised an eclectic mix of commercial and residential buildings that were each impressive in their own right but downright magnificent when beheld collectively. And over all of them soared the spectacular new One World Trade Center building.

"James's daughter."

"James has a *daughter*?"

Skylar nodded. "Can you believe it? Talk about killing two birds with one stone with this engagement. It's like 'wham bam thank you ma'am.' After being single your entire life, *boom*, you're about to be a wife *and* a stepmother."

"What's her name? How old is she?"

"Sloane. She's nineteen, goes to Columbia. God, that makes me feel old." Skylar stood up and walked toward the bar. "Anyone want some more wine? Or water?"

"Water please," Krissa said.

"Water for me too, thanks. Wow, a stepdaughter in college. So I take it she's not the warm-and-fuzzy type?" Daphne asked.

"You could say that," Skylar said as she handed them each a glass of water. "*Reserved* might be the best way to describe her."

"She's being way too nice," Krissa said to Daphne. "I've only seen her from afar, but from what I've heard, the girl's a straight-up bitch."

Skylar narrowed her eyes at Krissa. "Be nice. That's my future stepdaughter you're talking about."

"Just rendering a verdict based on the evidence that has been presented to me," Krissa said.

Skylar looked at Daphne. "She's not a bitch. She's just a little ... distant. But she definitely isn't a fan of yours truly. Her mom died when she was little, so I think she's used to having James all to herself. And let's be honest—it's not like I'm coming into the picture with a master's degree in parenting. What do I know about interacting with a teenager? I try to connect with her by telling her stories about my own college days, you know, to let her know that I remember what life is like at that age? But try as I might, we just don't seem to click."

"Don't sell yourself short. Your nieces and nephews adore you," Daphne said.

"True, but those kids are a lot younger, and there's a huge difference between being an aunt and being a stepmom. How does Emma get along with Brian's wife?"

"Okay, I guess. We don't really talk about it much, but I think Emma likes her. Actually, that's not true. I *know* she likes her. She probably even loves her now. I hate to admit that that bothers me, but it kind of does."

"Not that I have any personal experience to reference, but that sure sounds like a completely normal reaction to having another woman help raise your child," Skylar said.

"You have a daughter?" Krissa asked Daphne.

Daphne's face lit up. "Emma, my pride and joy. I used to call her my baby, but she's taller than I am now and will be a senior in high school this fall. I can't believe it."

"A senior in high school? Wow. You don't look old enough to have a daughter that age."

"I got married young," Daphne said. "Too young."

Krissa frowned. "I'm beginning to doubt I'll *ever* get married."

"And there's *nothing wrong* with that," Skylar said. "We've been through this a hundred times."

"Easy for you to say, with that five-pound rock attached to your hand."

Skylar chuckled. "Touché. I will stop talking now."

"You're not seeing anyone?" Daphne asked Krissa.

"I see people, just rarely the same guy more than once. If you're a single woman in your thirties, New York's like a dating wasteland."

"How could that be, with so many people here?"

"Oh it *be*, despite popular opinion among the coupled-up that finding love is as easy as picking out a piece of fruit. At least that's how it's been for me. If one more married or engaged person asks my why I'm still unattached, I literally might end up in jail on battery charges. To keep myself from throwing punches I've started saying it's because I have six toes on my left foot. You'd be amazed how many people immediately look at my feet when I say that, as if they really think that's why! I'd put it at ninety-nine percent, even when I'm wearing boots—give me a break! Sorry if I'm coming across a little bratty right now. It's been a long week."

"Krissa's a bit jaded about love, if you can't tell," Skylar said. "Although in my opinion she has every right to be." She threw a glance at Krissa. "Can I tell her?"

Krissa shrugged and took a sip of her water. "Why not?"

Skylar regained eye contact with Daphne. "A couple years ago her boyfriend got another woman pregnant. While they were *living together.*"

*"What?"* Daphne looked at Krissa, who nodded.

"Horrible, right? Now the jerk and his baby mama are apparently playing house somewhere in New Jersey," Skylar said.

"I actually don't think she's the baby mama anymore. I think she's the wife now, may they and their love child live happily ever after," Krissa said.

"Oh, damn him," Skylar said. "Good riddance."

"That's terrible, Krissa. I'm so sorry," Daphne said.

"Thanks. I'm over *him* now, thank God, but I'm not quite over *it*, as you can probably tell."

"Baby steps, honey. You'll get there," Skylar said.

"No wonder you're cynical about dating. If it's any consolation, I know how you feel. When Brian and I split up, I remember thinking that was it, that I'd be alone forever. I couldn't even imagine going out with someone new," Daphne said.

Skylar held up her water glass and clinked it against Daphne's. "Then you met not one, but *two* men on our trip to Saint Mirika. Talk about getting your groove back."

"You met *two* men on that trip?" Krissa said.

Daphne half smiled and cast her eyes downward.

Krissa turned and spoke to an imaginary judge. "Your Honor, let the record indicate that the witness has nonverbally answered in the affirmative. So who was the other guy?"

Daphne blushed. "He's actually the person I'm seeing now. His name's Derek."

"Also a hunk, though not as young," Skylar said. "Daphne had attractive men of all ages hitting on her that week and wisely chose not to discriminate based on birth year."

Krissa gave her an approving nod. "Girl, you done good. Way to bounce back with style. Is that in your book too?"

Daphne shook her head. "The book is only *loosely* based on our actual trip, despite what Skylar says."

"Well, loose or not, I want to read it. What's it called?"

"Um, right now it's called *Looking for Lexi*, but that's just a working title."

"*Looking for Lexi*, I like that. What's the Skylar character called in it?"

"In the book *mi nombre es* Sarah. That's literally the only thing I know how to say in Spanish besides *gracias* and *margarita, por favor.*"

Krissa reached for her phone. "Nice. I'm going to order a copy on Amazon right now. I'm always looking for a good read."

"Oh, it's not published," Daphne said.

"It's not?"

"It's not published *yet*, but it will be," Skylar said.

"It's just a manuscript for now," Daphne said.

*Probably forever.*

"Not for long. I read the entire thing on a flight to Paris and loved it, so I have no doubt that it will be coming to a book store near you soon," Skylar said.

"How soon?" Krissa asked.

"Yeah, any news on that front?" Skylar asked Daphne. "I can't wait to buy a bunch of copies and give them to every woman I know."

Daphne swallowed. "Not yet. Still waiting to hear back from some agents." Like her novel, that statement was also a thinly veiled version of the truth, but she was determined not to rain on the weekend's parade, which was about Skylar, not her. Besides, she *was* still waiting to hear back from two agents, which meant it *was* still possible that one would say yes. She no longer believed that wholeheartedly, but a tiny flame of hope still flickered somewhere deep inside her.

"Have you heard from any yet?" Skylar asked. "It seems like it's been a long time since you sent out the manuscript. Then again, my concept of time is clearly warped given that I didn't even know James six months ago—and look at me now."

"I've heard the publishing business is really hard to break into, a lot of hurry-up-and-wait and that sort of thing, so I'm not surprised it's taking a while," Krissa said.

Daphne buried her face in her water glass, trying to think of a way to shift the conversation without being too obvious about it. "Yeah, that's what I've heard too."

"I'm sure you'll hear something soon," Skylar said. "Maybe even this weekend. Wouldn't that be cool if they were all fighting over you and we got to see it play out? I'm really good at negotiating, so could totally help if you wanted me to."

"Thanks, Skylar." Daphne knew she had to change the subject before her poker face melted, so she turned and looked at Krissa. "I feel like we've been talking about *me* way too much. How about *you*? How did you meet Skylar?"

"Technically she's my client, although I've never actually worked on her account. I'm an attorney. We met at a work thing two, maybe three years ago now?" Krissa looked at Skylar to confirm.

"It'll be three years in September," Skylar said to Daphne. "I'll never forget it. I was walking out of the ladies' lounge at a fancy restaurant and Krissa literally sprinted across the room and grabbed me to tell me I had toilet paper stuck to the bottom of my heel."

"*I'd* want to know if I were in that situation, so I figured *she'd* want to know. And better to hear it from me than some guy, am I right?" Krissa said to Daphne.

Daphne laughed, grateful for the new direction the conversation had taken. "I'd *definitely* want to know."

"As did I," Skylar said. "Anyhow, after that bonding moment we became fast friends. Krissa's a badass too, as are all my gal pals. She's on the partner track at her firm."

Krissa patted her thighs. "I wish the track involved an *actual* track so I could get some exercise. Although, who am I kidding? I hate exercising. I probably wouldn't even work out if I worked *at* a gym."

Skylar laughed and looked at Daphne. "See why she and I get along so well? I found the only other woman in Manhattan who doesn't view sweating and feeling uncomfortable as a religion."

"Sedentary soul mates?" Daphne said.

"Totally," Krissa said, then craned her neck to have a look at her own backside. "God knows I *should* get off my bedonkadonk more. I've recently noticed that I have a serious case of office butt going on."

Skylar rolled her eyes. "Please. You're thirty-two. Your butt is fine."

"Maybe for now, but I see major squish action on the horizon," Krissa said.

Daphne looked in the direction of the elevator. "Hey, speaking of working out as a religion, where's KC? Shouldn't she be here by now?"

"Her flight was delayed, but I checked the status right before you got here and it said she'd landed, so it shouldn't be too much longer until she shows up. I told Stephen to send her directly up here," Skylar said.

"I take it KC doesn't suffer from office butt?" Krissa said.

"Quite the contrary," Skylar said. "I wouldn't be surprised if she's literally running here from the airport."

As if on cue, the elevator door opened and KC emerged, looking tired—and notably paler than Daphne was used to seeing her. As a fitness instructor who gave many of her classes on the beach, KC's golden tan was as much a part of her persona as her trademark blonde ponytail.

"Hey, guys," she offered a weary wave as she rolled her suitcase onto the deck. "Sorry I'm so late. My plane was delayed."

"As if that's your fault. Now come here and embrace me." Skylar stood up and wrapped her arms around tiny KC. "Krissa, this is KC, also known as the Third Musketeer."

Krissa stood up and shook KC's hand. "It's a pleasure. I hate to leave just when the party's getting started, but I really need to jet."

"You're not coming to dinner with us?" Daphne asked.

Krissa frowned. "I wish I could, but unfortunately I have a date."

"And you sound thrilled about it," Daphne said.

"I know, right? Is it that obvious?" Krissa said.

"If you were my attorney, you'd probably advise me not to answer that question," Daphne said.

"Well played," Krissa said with a nod.

KC stood there, looking confused. Daphne said she would fill her in after Krissa left.

"Who's this one with again?" Skylar asked Krissa. "I feel like you told me, but I'm blanking."

"His name is Eric. He's an English professor at NYU."

"That's right, the professor. I remember now. Stats?"

"Thirty-five, never been married, no kids but wants them someday, at least that's what it says in his profile. He's not gorgeous or anything, but then again let's face it, neither am I." She patted her cheek. "On that note, how do I look? Is it painfully evident that I spend most of my waking hours swathed in the dim glow of fluorescent office lighting? I really need to buy some bronzing powder."

"You look great. He'll adore you. And if he doesn't, he's an idiot and it's on to the next one," Skylar said.

"Thanks for the vote of confidence." Krissa waved to the three of them as she stepped into the elevator. "It was nice meeting the other two Musketeers. Daphne, best of luck with the book. KC, I'm sorry we didn't get a chance to chat. Skylar, thanks for the happy juice. I'll see all three of you later this weekend, I hope."

Skylar blew her a kiss. "You'd better. Good luck tonight, hon."

Daphne waved to Krissa as the elevator door closed, then looked at Skylar. "I really like her. She seems feisty, but in a good way."

"Isn't she great? And you're right on the money about the feistiness. I love being on her good side but would hate to be on her bad side."

"Hmm. Sounds like someone you know, perhaps? Like *yourself?*" Daphne said.

"Fair enough. I told you, I'm very selective about those I chose to invite into the inner circle, which is why it's such an exclusive club." Skylar smoothed a hand over KC's ponytail. "Now, what can I get *you* to drink before we head out to dinner? We have pretty much everything, so name your poison. Daphne and I are drinking chardonnay, but now that I think of it, I should have made some vodka appletinis to welcome you both to the Big Apple."

"A vodka appletini? I've never heard of that," Daphne said.

"It's both refreshing *and* delicious. Plus I didn't eat any fruit today, so I'm also calling it *nutritious*."

"I like the way you justify your beverage choices," Daphne said. "Impressive verbal gymnastics too. That was like a little poem."

"Why thank you. So what can I get you, my little peanut? You're awfully quiet." Skylar said to KC.

"Just water for me. Thanks Skylar. I'm pretty beat."

Skylar glanced at her watch. "Do either of you want to take a shower before dinner, or are you good? We have a little time before our reservation, so it's up to you."

"Is the restaurant far from here?" Daphne asked.

"Not too far, maybe a ten-minute cab ride."

"Do you ride the subway a lot?" KC asked. "I saw a station right by your apartment."

"Never. I take cabs everywhere."

"Even to work?" Daphne asked.

"Yep. My motto is 'Why take a crowded, dirty subway train when you can ride in a clean, air-conditioned car?'"

*Sounds like an expensive motto*, Daphne thought.

KC yawned. "Do you think maybe I could take a quick power nap? I hate to be a party pooper, but I'm exhausted."

"Sure, nap away. Let's get you both settled in the guest rooms downstairs."

As they followed Skylar into the elevator, Daphne tapped a noticeably subdued KC on the arm. "You doing okay?" she whispered to her typically bubbly friend.

KC yawned again. "Just a little tired."

# Chapter Seven

"How did you and James meet? You said he was a client or something like that?" Daphne asked Skylar as they finished up dinner. The three of them were in the trendy Chelsea neighborhood at da Umberto, an upscale Italian spot that Daphne feared was going to put a significant dent in her budget. She was trying not to focus on money but was concerned about how much she'd be spending if Skylar kept choosing restaurants—and wine—as nice as this one.

"Yep. His company uses our software, but he's miles removed from that sort of thing, so it's kind of a miracle that our paths crossed because of it. We met at a work-related event that had nothing to do with either company—other than the fact that we were both sponsoring it in some way or another, I'm not even sure how. Anyhow, it was the typical Manhattan setting, a cocktail-party-fundraiser thing. As you may have already realized, there is a *lot* of drinking that goes on in this town. My tolerance has been holding steady at an all-time high for years now."

"I can't remember the last time I went to a cocktail party," Daphne said, then looked at KC. "Do you and Max go to a lot of cocktail parties?"

"I can't remember the last time I *had* a cocktail," KC said. "I loved that movie, though. Remember? With Tom Cruise and what's-her-face with the brother who was on *Melrose Place*?"

"Elisabeth Shue," Daphne said.

KC lifted her palm to Daphne's for a high five. "Good memory. Such a talented actress. I loved her in *Leaving Las Vegas*. But no, Max and I don't go to a lot of cocktail parties. And now that I think of it, I'm pretty sure the last cocktail I had was in Saint Mirika."

"Ah yes, the rum punches. You were downing those like it was End Times," Daphne said.

"I love watching you when you're drunk. It makes me happy," Skylar said.

"It doesn't happen very often, that's for sure," KC said. "It's hard to get up at six for a workout when you have a hangover."

"I know what you mean. I *hate* being hungover, especially when I have to wake up early the next day and be Mom. I rarely have more than one glass of wine anymore," Daphne said.

Skylar rolled her eyes. "You two are way too healthy for New York. Here's a story that will give you an idea of what life is like here. A woman who works for me said that at her son's preschool, the kids were invited to bring things in from home for arts and crafts, like every Friday or something, and after the first few weeks the principal sent an e-mail out to all the parents saying please, *please*, no more corks. That about sums up parenting in Manhattan: a lot of empty wine bottles!" She chuckled and refilled her glass, as well as

Daphne's, with the bottle of cabernet she'd selected for the table.

KC had decided to abstain from alcohol for the evening, saying it would only make her more tired.

"Actually, that reminds me of *another* story. This other woman I work with told me that when she and her husband were interviewing for preschools—people have to do that here, *interview* for preschools, can you imagine?—anyhow, when they were interviewing, or when their *son* was interviewing, I should say, because they interview the kids too, scary as that is, they were at this one school and he had to interact with a bunch of other kids in a little play area. I guess that's how they evaluate their social skills, maturity level, etc. So anyhow, there was this one section with a bunch of play furniture like a house, and you'll never guess what their kid did—with *all the administrators* watching with their clipboards and snooty attitudes."

"Do we want to know?" Daphne said.

"Apparently he made a beeline to the kitchen area, pulled out some plastic cups from a cabinet, and announced he was making cocktails."

KC's jaw dropped. "No way."

"Isn't that amazing? My coworker and her husband were mortified of course, but you know what? *That* was the only school their kid got into, literally the only one. God, I love New York."

"Raising kids here must be a challenge," Daphne said. "Where do they run around if no one has a backyard?"

"I have no idea. Parks, I guess? I've managed to live a lifestyle that prevents me from coming into contact with anyone too young to work in an office—or a bar. Until Sloane came along, that is. Although I do see a ton of baby strollers, so I know they're out there. I just don't notice them, kind of like white noise."

"Max has a white noise machine to sleep," KC said. "His favorite setting is 'ocean breeze.'"

"I have one of those too!" Daphne said. "I like 'forest dreams.'"

"James uses a fan for white noise," Skylar said. "Even in the wintertime. He puts it on facing away from the bed. It drives me nuts, but he hates that I wear a night guard, so I guess we're even."

"What's a night guard?" KC asked.

Skylar squeezed her jaw. "It's kind of like a retainer. I grind my teeth when I sleep, so it basically keeps me from cracking them."

"Yikes!" KC said. "That doesn't sound fun."

"It's not bad. It's a little awkward at first, but once you get used to it, it's almost like a pacifier."

"Do you grind your teeth because of stress?" Daphne asked.

"Probably. Who knows? I've been doing it for years."

"I wear earplugs," KC said. "Max snores like a beast sometimes."

"I wear an eye mask *and* earplugs, even when I sleep alone," Daphne said.

Skylar groaned. "Can we please change the subject? We sound like old women."

"Fair enough. So you were saying that you and James met at a cocktail party?" Daphne said.

"Yes. This will give you a sense of his personality. I'd just finished chatting with a coworker who had gone off to the restroom, and James walked right up to me and asked if he could buy me a drink. I was like, 'Uh, it's an open bar.' He just smiled at me."

Daphne laughed. "That's clever."

"Isn't it? Then he told me he'd been watching me all night and knew he'd kick himself if he didn't come over and dazzle me with his sparkling wit before he missed his chance." She chuckled. "Those were his exact words, *dazzle* and *sparkling wit*. He's kind of a cheese ball, but a sweet cheese ball."

KC put a hand over her heart. "Aw, that's such a cute story. Like in the movies. I can't wait to meet him."

"I'm so happy for you, Skylar. He sounds like a keeper," Daphne said.

Skylar smiled. "I think so too. He's super funny, but also very romantic and genuine. Plus he's sharp as a tack, which keeps me on my toes."

"Is he as smart as you?" KC asked. "I don't think I know anyone as smart as you."

"Please. I'm not *that* smart," Skylar said.

*Tell that to the zillion people who work for you,* Daphne thought.

"Anyhow, we ended up chatting for the entire party. It was almost as if no one else were in the room—kind of freaky, but that's how it seemed. And then before we knew it the party was over and nearly everyone was gone. He walked me all the way home and we talked nonstop the entire way, although I can't remember what we talked about because I was so giddy. Can you imagine? Me? Giddy?"

"You seem pretty giddy right now," Daphne said.

Skylar twirled the stem of her wine glass. "I'll take that. Anyhow, when we got to my building—that's when I was living in the West Village—he kissed me on the cheek and asked if he could buy me a drink for real the next time. I took the elevator back up to my apartment, but I probably could have floated up there if I wanted to. I don't think I slept a wink that night. Then he called me the next day, and the day after that, and the day after that, and every day since."

"Wow! I've never heard you talk like this, Skylar," KC said.

Skylar nibbled on her thumbnail. "I know. It's terrible, right? I'm totally smitten. It's kind of out of control."

"It's adorable," Daphne said. "How did he propose?"

Skylar's face lit up. "It was completely unexpected. But before I tell you the story, can I interest either of you in dessert? The tiramisu here is to die for."

Daphne shook her head. "Sorry, I'm stuffed."

"I'll have some," KC said.

"Great, we can split it." Skylar motioned for the waiter. "After we finish we can take a walk on the High Line before heading home. It's not too far from here."

"What's the High Line?" Daphne asked.

"It's a narrow bridge between two skyscrapers, but with no railing, so it's kind of dicey," Skylar said with a straight face.

"What?" KC's eyes turned to saucers.

"I'm kidding. It's an old elevated rail track they turned into a really cool park that winds through the streets, actually *above* the streets, so you can look down as you walk. It's a very creative use of the space. I warn you that it might be a little crowded, though. It's kind of everyone's favorite thing to do these days."

"Count me in," Daphne said. "I need to walk off that dinner, although KC will probably want to jog hers off."

She looked at KC, expecting a reaction, but KC seemed distracted and didn't respond.

When the waiter returned with the dessert a few moments later, Skylar handed him her credit card. "Dinner is on me, so don't even think about reaching for your wallets," she said to her friends.

"But Skylar—" Daphne said.

"No arguing," Skylar said with a firm smile. "Your money is no good here. Now let's enjoy this deliciousness. I'll tell you the proposal story on our walk."

# Chapter Eight

"Wow, how cool is this?" KC's eyes grew wide after they ascended the stairs on Twenty-Third Street leading to the High Line. "It really used to be a train track?"

"Yep. Amazing, isn't it? For years it was just sitting here abandoned, doing nothing but collecting rust and dust and basically acting as a major eyesore. Now it's a Manhattan treasure," Skylar said.

Daphne peered up and down the walkway, which was lined with plants, trees, shrubs, flower patches, sturdy wood benches, and matching reclining chairs—all amid old tracks. "I can understand why. I've never seen anything like it. It's like a sprawling backyard deck combined with a nursery—the kind where they sell plants, of course, not the baby kind. How long is it?"

"I'm not sure. They keep expanding it. Maybe a mile, a mile and a half now? KC could probably sprint to the end of it before I make it to that bench over there," Skylar said.

Daphne smiled and looked at KC to see her response, but KC was staring off into the distance again and appeared not to have heard.

The three of them began walking south, blending into a river of pedestrians who had entered the park at a different access point.

When they came to a clearing in the pathway a few blocks later, Daphne turned to Skylar. "So let's hear the proposal story."

Skylar's countenance brightened, adding a sparkle to her eyes. The thought of James obviously did something special to her. "We were at his place one rainy Sunday afternoon, on the Upper East Side, just chilling on the couch, drinking red wine, and eating popcorn and watching a movie. That's our favorite thing to do when the weather's bad. Anyhow, it was dumping cats and dogs outside that day and the forecast said it was supposed to pour the entire next day as well, so I made a comment about how I wished I'd brought my raincoat and boots over to his place so I wouldn't have to take a cab all the way back to my apartment to get them before going to work the next morning. I didn't even look at him when I said it. All of a sudden, the TV was on mute. I turned to ask him what had happened to the sound, and he looked at me with this silly grin and said, 'I wish you wouldn't go back to your place ever again.' At first I thought he was just asking me to move in with him, which was big enough, but then he got down on one knee. I started crying, and the rest is history."

"I just got chills," Daphne said.

"What a romantic guy," KC said.

"How did Max propose?" Skylar asked KC. "I don't think I ever heard that story."

"I can't remember exactly. I think one day we just decided to get married."

Daphne looked at her. "That's it? That's your engagement story?"

"Hey don't knock it. They're *still* married, which is the important part," Skylar said.

"Touché," Daphne said. She could recite her own fairy-tale engagement story like the best of them. What did that prove? Nothing, apparently. She glanced at Skylar's enormous diamond and ran a thumb over her own ring finger, bare now for several years.

Skylar checked her watch and pointed to a staircase leading down to West Fourteenth Street. "I'm thinking we take that exit and grab a cab to my place so we can hit the hay. We have a big day ahead of us tomorrow, and I'm sure Wonder Woman here wants to run about twenty miles before breakfast."

Daphne and Skylar both looked at KC, expecting a witty reply. But KC just stared ahead, gazing into the distance.

Skylar waved a hand in front of KC's face. "Hello? Earth to KC."

KC blinked. "I'm sorry. What did you say?"

"I said it's time to head back to my place to get some sleep. You seem to be in need of a lot of that today."

"Oh, got it. Sure, let's go home," KC said.

"Are you okay?" Daphne asked her.

"I'm fine," she said with an unconvincing smile.

"You sure?"

"Yep. Still just a little tired."

Daphne decided to let it go and began making her way toward the exit alongside KC, but Skylar had other ideas. She stepped in front of them and put her hands on her hips.

"No," she said to KC.

"I'm sorry?" KC said.

"I said no. I've seen you be your bubbly self a million times despite barely having slept a wink, so I'm not buying that you're acting like this because you're tired, especially given that you already took a nap. Now, what's really going on with you? You've been acting weird since you got here. Am I right, Daphne?"

Daphne looked at KC and gave her an apologetic nod. "You do seem a little off."

KC stood there for a moment, averting her gaze. As a wave of locals and tourists wandered by them, a mixture of all ages out to enjoy an evening stroll in the balmy New York weather, Daphne and Skylar exchanged a worried glance. They'd never seen KC like this. With a start, Daphne realized that something wasn't just off, something was *wrong*.

"KC, are you *really* okay?" Daphne said.

KC didn't answer.

"KC, honey?" Skylar said, her voice suddenly softer. "What's going on?"

KC shook her head, still not making eye contact. "This is your weekend, Skylar. I don't want it to be about me."

Daphne felt the hair on the back of her neck stand up. Could something *really* be wrong? "Okay, now you're scaring me," she said.

Skylar reached for KC's hand, a concerned expression on her face now matching the tone of her voice. "Me too. KC, babe, please tell us what's going on."

KC continued to stare off into the distance. After a long pause, she sighed and finally gestured to a nearby bench. "Can we sit down for a minute?"

"Of course," Skylar said. She and Daphne followed KC to the bench, and the three of them quietly took a seat, KC in the middle, staring straight ahead. Daphne and Skylar exchanged another worried glance.

After a few moments of uncomfortable silence, KC spoke. "For several weeks now I haven't been feeling that well, so Max finally convinced me to go to the doctor."

A cold shiver ran down Daphne's spine.

"They did some blood work," KC said.

Daphne began to feel light-headed.

*This can't be happening. This can't be happening.*

She kicked herself for having been so caught up in her own self-pity about her book when KC was clearly facing something far more serious.

"And ...?" Skylar asked.

KC didn't respond, and Daphne's mind continued to race. KC was the healthiest person she'd ever met. She braced herself for the one word she didn't want to hear. The one word no one wanted to hear after the phrase "they did some blood work." She leaned back against the bench for support.

"KC, what did they find out?" Skylar asked.

After what seemed like an eternity, KC closed her eyes and took a deep breath, then opened them again.

"Well, it turns out I'm fine. Just mildly anemic. And pregnant."

*"What?"* Skylar stood up.

"Oh my God!" Daphne covered her mouth with her hand. "Way to bury the lede!"

KC smiled and made a *what can you do?* motion with her hands. "My friends, I am officially with child."

Skylar lightly punched KC in the arm. "I thought you were going to say you had cancer! I thought you were dying!" She looked at Daphne. "Did you think she was dying?"

Daphne nodded and gave KC a gentle shove. "I totally thought you were dying. You really need to rethink your delivery."

The look on KC's face turned sheepish. "Oh man, I'm sorry, guys. I didn't mean to scare you. I wasn't planning to say anything, but you kind of squeezed it out of me."

"You weren't planning to tell us?" Skylar said as she sat back down. "You mean like *all weekend?*"

KC shook her head.

"Why in the world not? You should have told us the moment we saw you," Daphne said.

Skylar looked at her watch. "Seriously! How could you keep news that big to yourself for what, *four hours* now?"

"I didn't want to steal your thunder, Skylar. We're here to celebrate *you*, not me."

Skylar laughed and patted KC's head. "Oh hon, you really are the nicest person alive. They should make a cartoon character out of you. Have I said that before?"

KC grinned. "Once or twice."

"Wow! Pregnant. I did *not* see that one coming," Daphne said with a whistle. "Talk about a plot twist."

"Was it planned?" Skylar asked.

"Skylar!" Daphne said.

"What? This is the inner circle, remember? Nothing is off-limits. I've never heard KC talk about wanting to have kids, but it's not like women our age get pregnant at the drop of a hat. It's usually with the help of a pharmacist."

"It wasn't really *planned*, but it wasn't *unplanned* either," KC said. "And no pharmacist was involved."

Skylar held up a finger. "Let me guess, you fell in love with—what's your step-granddaughter's name again?"

"Julia."

"You fell in love with adorable little Julia and decided to pull the goalie to let Mother Nature make the decision for you. Am I right?"

KC blushed. "Maybe."

Skylar tapped her temple. "Me know things."

"When I married a man with kids of his own I thought that would be enough for me, but I guess I changed my mind. Plus I've missed those boys like crazy since they moved out, so it's not as much a matter of having my *own* kid as having *another* kid around," KC said.

"And that's why Max never got snipped? Just in case one day you changed your mind?" Skylar asked.

Daphne looked at her. "Snipped?"

Skylar made scissors with her fingers. "You know, snip, down there …"

Daphne laughed. "Love the euphemism. I hadn't heard that one before."

"Yes, that's why he never got *snipped*. It was his idea, actually. He's pretty smart about women," KC said.

"I'd say so. I can see why you keep him around," Daphne said.

"What does *he* think about Mother Nature's decision to bring another bundle of joy into the house?" Skylar asked.

"Once he got used to the idea of going down that road again, especially at his age, he came around," KC said. "He's pretty excited about it now."

"How old is he?" Daphne asked.

"Fifty-four."

"*Nice,*" Skylar said with a nod. "You know deep down he's patting himself on the back."

KC laughed. "He has made a few comments about how his boys can still swim."

Skylar pulled KC's ponytail. "I still can't believe you would keep something this important to yourself for fear of stealing *my* thunder. I couldn't give a rat's ass about my thunder."

"But your getting engaged is a huge deal too, and I didn't want to make this weekend about me. I'm so happy for you, Skylar. Really, just thrilled."

"Thanks, babe, but there's plenty of room in this weekend for more than one thunder," Skylar looked at Daphne. "And for the record, I realize that was terrible syntax. Or grammar. Or whatever the word is."

Daphne smiled. "It's been a long night. I'll let it slide."

KC looked at her hands. "Also, there's another reason I didn't want to bring it up."

"Is the baby okay?" Daphne asked.

"Yes, yes, as far as I know the baby's fine. Although it's still so early. Anyhow, when I found out I was pregnant I couldn't help but remember what you two were saying on the video call we had last month. You know, when Daphne thought Skylar might be expecting?"

"What did we say?" Skylar said. "I have no memory of that."

"I can't remember exactly how you put it, but it was something about how if you *were* pregnant, your baby could have play dates with Julia, like that would be totally crazy or something," KC said.

"We said that?" Daphne said.

KC nodded.

Daphne gave KC a rueful look. "I'm sorry. Would you believe me if I said we were kidding?"

KC smiled. "We all know you weren't kidding. It's okay, but that's another reason why I was reluctant to bring it up. I guess I was a little embarrassed to be pregnant at this age, especially when I already have a granddaughter. I guess I *am* a little embarrassed."

Skylar put a hand on KC's shoulder. "*We're* the ones who should be embarrassed. We were just being mean girls. Lots of women in their forties have babies these days, and lots of men in their fifties become fathers. The important thing is how *you* feel about it, and Max too, of course. Are you happy? Nervous?"

"Both, I guess. I'm still trying to wrap my head around the idea of being a mom, not just a stepmom when they're already in high school. A mom from day one."

"Understandable," Daphne said. "I remember feeling a whole jumble of emotions when I found out I was pregnant with Emma." She didn't want to mention that one of them was fear, given the multiple miscarriages she'd suffered before she'd been able to carry her daughter to term. That was the last thing KC needed to hear right now.

KC yawned and stretched her arms over her head. "What I'm *really* feeling right now is extreme fatigue. So now that my cat is out of the bag, can we please go back to Skylar's and pick up this conversation tomorrow? I'm dying for some shut-eye."

Skylar tugged KC's ponytail again. "Do not say 'I'm dying' in my presence ever again."

KC laughed. "Oops, my bad. Sorry, pals."

# Chapter Nine

Daphne woke up early the next morning and wandered around the quiet apartment in her pajamas, trying to quell the growing feeling of inadequacy tugging at her as she marveled at its grandeur. Skylar was right in that the place was sparsely decorated, but what was there was beautiful—and clearly high-end. The living room was done in neutral shades, the only hint of color lying in boldly striped blue-and-yellow pillows placed just so on the taupe leather couches. Everything was in its place, not a speck of dust on the end tables or hardwood floors, the sleek area rugs perfectly aligned.

Daphne couldn't remember the last time she'd bought new furniture of any kind for her own modest house, which she'd been granted in the divorce. She'd briefly toyed with the idea of selling it to give herself a fresh start, most likely downsizing to a condo to reduce her living expenses, but she'd decided to wait until Emma left for college to do so. She hated that she relied on alimony and child support from Brian to supplement her part-time wages from the flower store, despite his insistence that she was entitled to every penny. She knew the arrangement was fair and that having forgone a career for her family was nothing to be ashamed of, but that didn't make it any easier to see how wealthy Skylar had become during the years Daphne had spent raising Emma.

*Could I have achieved the same level of professional success if I'd pursued it with the ardor that Skylar did?*

She wasn't so sure. In Daphne's opinion, it was more than hard work that had gotten Skylar to where she was. Skylar had something special about her that Daphne had always overtly admired while secretly envying.

Not wanting to wake her friends, Daphne retrieved her phone from the guest bedroom, then quietly made her way into the kitchen. She took a seat at a stool alongside the island and logged into her e-mail account. The night before, she'd altered the settings on her phone so it wouldn't push e-mail and potentially ruin her weekend with more bad news about her book. But here she was, actively asking to be disappointed again.

*Or maybe elated?*

She held her breath when she saw that she had a new message—from an agent—and immediately clicked to open it.

*Dear Daphne, thank you for submitting* Looking for Lexi *for my review. While I believe the story has promise, unfortunately I don't think it's the right fit for my list at this time. I wish you the best of luck finding representation.*

Daphne sighed and set the phone on the counter. That brought the tally to thirty-five rejections. Only one agent left. She already regretted having checked her e-mail.

*Why did I do that to myself? Why couldn't I have let myself at least try to enjoy the rest of the weekend with my friends?*

Sitting alone in Skylar's magazine-worthy kitchen, tiny pricks of self-doubt again began nipping at Daphne's heels. She interlaced her hands in her lap and squeezed them tight, willing herself to stay positive—not just for herself, but for Skylar and KC, who didn't need to see her wallowing in self-pity.

In an effort to focus on something else, she thought of the news KC had shared last night and pictured her cradling a tiny baby boy or girl. Daphne knew that little person would be extremely lucky to have KC as a mother. She didn't share KC's concern that she might be too old for motherhood, but she did wonder what it would be like to have a baby at this age. Back when Daphne had become a mother, she had been practically a child herself and was often overwhelmed by the responsibility of taking care of another human being.

*Would I have been a better mother to Emma with more life experience under my belt?*

It was a question with no answer, much like wondering what her life would have been like if she'd chosen to go to college in New York, or to pursue a career here after graduation instead of staying in Chicago, where she'd quickly met Brian.

*And what about now? Would I ever consider having another child? With Derek, if our relationship progressed to that point?*

At the thought of him she realized that she still hadn't called or even texted him to tell him that she'd made it safely to New York. She felt a pinch of guilt.

*Should I call him now? No, he might be sleeping.*

She'd reach out to him later, although she didn't feel like filling him in on the latest news about her manuscript. The truth was she didn't want to tell *anyone*, especially Skylar. For now, at least, Skylar steadfastly believed in Daphne's abilities as a writer.

*If she knew how many agents had turned me down, how would her opinion of me change? Would she lose respect for me? Feel sorry for me?*

Daphne didn't want her friend to pity her—she couldn't stand pity. She balled her hands into fists, frustrated by how quickly she'd returned to thinking about the book.

"Well, good morning, sunshine! I thought you might sleep in because you're on vacation. Can I brew you some coffee?"

Daphne looked up to see Skylar stroll into the kitchen wearing a short green nightgown and matching robe, a pair of fluffy white slippers on her feet.

"Hey Skylar, good morning to you too. Coffee sounds great, thanks. I'm not sure why I woke up so early. Habit, I guess. I haven't slept in since before Emma was born."

"Whatcha reading?"

Daphne glanced at her phone. "Just scanning the headlines." She knew she should come clean about the rejection, about *all* the rejections, but she couldn't bring herself to bring it up. Besides, she didn't want to drag down Skylar's sunny spirits.

To Daphne's relief, before Skylar could ask her any more questions KC walked into the kitchen carrying a small pink gift bag. "Morning," she said with a yawn.

"Looks like KC's the real early bird today, given the time change," Daphne said.

KC was wearing white shorts and a light blue T-shirt that said "Summer Is a State of Mind." Daphne noticed that they were regular shorts, not the kind worn for exercise. Skylar noticed too and narrowed her eyes. "What's with the outfit?"

"What do you mean?" KC asked.

"I think she means why aren't you dressed in workout clothes?" Daphne asked.

Skylar pointed at Daphne. "What she said. It's the morning. You're *always* dressed in workout clothes in the morning. Sometimes I've wondered if you *sleep* in workout clothes."

Daphne laughed. "I've wondered that too."

KC set the pink bag on the counter. "I thought I'd take it easy on the exercise this weekend, especially since we're already going to be walking around so much."

"But what about our run in Central Park? I thought you were looking forward to that. *I* was even looking forward to that," Daphne said.

"I'm sorry. Maybe you can go by yourself?" KC said.

Daphne shot a confused glance at Skylar, who returned the look, then said, "Okay KC, spill it. What's the real reason you don't want to run? You might as well just tell us. After last night, I would have thought that you'd learned your lesson about keeping secrets from the inner circle."

KC climbed onto a kitchen stool. "Okay, fine. The truth is, I don't want to hurt the baby."

"Hurt the baby? What are you, like a week pregnant?" Skylar said.

"Seven weeks. The doctor says I'm a high-risk pregnancy because of my age, so I don't want to do anything that might jeopardize it." She patted her belly, which Daphne knew was probably flat and toned underneath that T-shirt.

"Did the doctor say no running?" Daphne asked.

"Not specifically," KC said.

"How long have you known you're expecting?" Skylar asked.

"About a month."

"Have you exercised at all since then?" Daphne asked.

"Not really."

"*Not really* meaning …" Skylar said.

"Okay, not at all," KC said, a resigned look on her face. "But that's okay. I'll manage."

"It seems a little extreme to cut out exercise entirely, especially given how much you normally work out," Daphne said. "It's not like your body isn't used to it or anything."

"I don't want to take any chances," KC said.

"I'd gladly give up exercising if I got pregnant. Giving up alcohol would be the hard part," Skylar said.

Daphne and KC both laughed at Skylar's joke, then Daphne caught Skylar's eye. She could tell that Skylar was thinking the same thing that she was: Was going cold turkey really necessary, especially for someone in extraordinary physical shape like KC? KC loved exercise.

As far as Daphne knew, she'd gone for a run nearly every day of her life.

*But who am I to judge my friend's choices?*

Daphne had been pregnant in her early twenties, not her early forties, so she had a much different perspective. She decided to change the subject to something less touchy. "So what's on the agenda for today?" she asked Skylar.

"First up is food, which I guess we can do earlier rather than later now that Super Girl here is acting mortal for once." She reached for her phone. "I'll ask Krissa if she wants to join us, although given how early it is she might think I'm nuts. No one goes to brunch this early in New York, but we have a big day ahead of us."

"I wonder how her date went last night," Daphne said.

Skylar tapped out a message. "We'll find out soon enough. I *love* her dating stories. A couple weeks ago she went out with a guy who mentioned in the middle of their first drink that he was nervous because he hadn't had sex in three years."

Daphne cringed. "Ouch. Not that there's anything wrong with a dry spell of course, but I'm not sure I would recommend putting it out there that fast, if at all."

"My thoughts exactly." Skylar pointed to the bag in front of KC. "Got another cat in there? Although I'm not sure how you could top the news about the bun you've got cooking in the oven."

"Just a little gift for my two besties. But you'll have to wait."

76

"Again with you and the secrets! So mysterious," Skylar said. Just then her phone beeped with a text. She picked it up and laughed out loud at the message.

"What's so funny?" Daphne asked.

Skylar turned the phone around and held it out for them to read. "It's a text from Krissa. I guess her date didn't go so well."

KC and Daphne peered at the screen.

*He showed up wearing one of those T-shirts with a tuxedo printed on it. Game over.*

# Chapter Ten

Daphne, Skylar, and KC were just finishing up breakfast at Edward's on West Broadway when Skylar elbowed Daphne and nodded in the direction of Krissa, who was approaching them—looking notably disheveled.

"Look what the cat dragged in. Glad you made it. Have a seat." Skylar scooted over in the booth.

Krissa plopped down next to her. "Sorry I'm so late, and yes I realize that I look like yesterday's lunch heated up in the microwave. I didn't get much sleep."

"Are you hungry?" KC asked Krissa. "We already ate, but I think I'm going to order some more bacon and maybe a pancake. The food here is super yummy."

"Nah, I'm good. I had two enormous slices of pizza at like four in the morning."

"Why were you out so late? I thought the date was a bust. I showed the girls your text, by the way. Yowsa," Skylar said.

"Brutal, right? Welcome to my world, Daphne and KC. Anyhow, after the date imploded I met up with some younger friends for a drink that turned into a *few* drinks, and somehow we ended up at a club in Williamsburg. I think I was the oldest person there by at least five years."

She reached for Skylar's water glass. "Can I have some of this? I'm super dehydrated."

"Hydrate away." Skylar looked at Daphne and KC. "Williamsburg's the hipster part of Brooklyn. You two would hate it. Not Brooklyn, just Williamsburg."

Daphne took a sip of coffee. "What's a hipster?"

"People who spend a lot of time making it look like they just rolled out of bed," Krissa said. "Unlike yours truly, who *did* just roll out of bed."

Skylar petted Krissa's rumpled hair. "Hey, you made it here, which is all that matters. I'm sorry your date with the professor was a bust. I know you were looking forward to that one."

"Eh, easy come, easy go. I'll get over it. Actually, on the subway here I made plans to meet another guy later today."

"Already?" Daphne said.

"I have a dating app on my phone," Krissa said. "Actually, I probably have *all* of the dating apps on my phone."

"She's a dating machine," Skylar said. "Reminds me a little bit of my former self."

"Who's today's date with?" KC asked.

"A guy named Alan who works in real estate and lives in Cobble Hill."

"Cobble Hill?" Daphne said.

"That's in Brooklyn too, but a much cuter part— from what I've heard," Skylar said. "I've never actually been to any of these places, mind you."

"Anyhow, I can't say I'm super jazzed by his photos, but he doesn't have any cat pics, so at least there's that," Krissa said.

"What's wrong with cats? I love cats," KC said.

Krissa shook her head. "I don't mean photos of him *with* a cat, I mean photos of *just* a cat. Big difference."

"Oh, I see your point." KC made a creeped-out face.

"What are you doing on your date?" Daphne asked.

Krissa sighed. "The usual. Meeting for a drink. All these first dates have basically turned me into an alcoholic."

"At least you're getting out there," KC said. "That's what you have to do, right?"

Skylar pressed a palm against her forehead. "Uh oh, here it comes."

"Here what comes?" Daphne asked.

Skylar cocked her head in the direction of Krissa. "The Speech."

"The Speech?" Daphne raised her eyebrows.

"Yes, ladies, prepare to hear The Speech. Krissa, you have the stage."

Krissa cleared her throat, then held up two fingers. "Single women looking for a relationship are bombarded with advice from two camps: Those who offer words of wisdom such as 'You need to put yourself out there! You need to be open to it!' and those who preach the exact opposite, or 'You can't be looking for it! It will happen when you least expect it!' On behalf of single women everywhere, I want to lock both camps in a windowless room and let them battle it out so they can get their story straight. And for the record, after all this dating I'm coming to the conclusion that love is completely random. There's no rhyme nor reason whatsoever to where we'll find it, or how. We'll drive ourselves crazy if we keep trying to figure it out, because when it comes down to it, it's all about timing, chemistry and *luck—* good or bad." She exhaled and took a sip of water.

Skylar held out her arm, game-show style. "There you have it, folks, The Speech."

"That was like a sermon," Daphne said with a laugh.

"It needs to go viral, don't you think?" Krissa said. "I could become a YouTube sensation."

• • •

After they left the restaurant, Skylar, who had again insisted on picking up the check, turned to her friends and put her hands on her waist. "So, I have an appointment for us to look at wedding dresses, but I was thinking it might be fun to go on a quick ferry ride first. I know it's super touristy, but it would be an easy way to see a lot of scenery in a short amount of time, plus that breeze would sure feel good on a hot day like today."

KC raised her hand. "I'm in! I love touristy!"

Krissa ran a finger across her neck. "I'm out. I would literally rather kill myself. I also need to take a marathon nap if I want to get rid of these bags under my eyes before my date. What's on the docket for tomorrow? Maybe I can join the nonbachelorette party again."

"Agenda's still TBD, but I'll text you," Skylar said.

"Sounds good." Krissa bade the trio goodbye, then headed toward the Chambers Street subway station.

"I really like her," Daphne said as they began walking in the other direction. "So straightforward, you know? Like a breath of fresh air."

"Isn't she great? Not an ounce of pretention in her bones. And she has me dying laughing with some of her dating stories. I bet she'll have a good one for us tomorrow," Skylar said.

As they began to walk along the sidewalk, a group of rollerbladers came barreling down the bike lane, and Daphne did a double-take as they approached. One of the men, dressed in navy board shorts and a yellow T-shirt, looked a *lot* like Clay Hanson.

*Could it be?*

She froze and stood there with her mouth half-open as he flew by. He was wearing sunglasses so she couldn't be sure, but the sudden increase in her heart rate, despite the fact that she was standing still, surprised her.

She watched the group recede in the distance, then caught up with Skylar and KC. Before she could tell them what had just happened, Skylar stopped walking. "Damn it, I left my phone back at the apartment. Do you mind if we swing by there for a minute?"

"Not at all," Daphne said, still a little rattled.

"I have to pee anyway," KC said.

"Cool, let's go." They turned around, but as soon as Skylar made a left onto her street, she froze. "Oh jeez, there she is," she said under her breath, her voice taking on a nervous quality that Daphne had never heard before. KC and Daphne stopped too.

"There's who?" KC looked at Skylar, then at Daphne. "Everyone I know in New York is standing right here."

"Sloane, James's daughter," Skylar said, her voice still hushed. "Do I look okay?"

"Are you joking? You look way better than okay," KC said.

Daphne couldn't agree more—and could hardly believe her ears. Skylar was really concerned about her appearance? Even now, out for a casual Saturday brunch, she was a picture of chic in a cream-colored sheath dress, a small emerald pendant dangling on a delicate gold chain around her neck. The robin-blue sundress Daphne wore was one of her favorites, but she knew it paled in comparison to Skylar's designer frock. KC was still in a T-shirt and shorts, her hair pulled back in a ponytail.

"KC's right, Skylar. You *always* look good," Daphne said.

"Thanks, ladies. I needed that." Skylar composed herself, then resumed a confident stride toward the building—and the young woman who had just exited it. Daphne and KC followed closely behind.

Daphne tried not to stare at Sloane as they approached her, but it wasn't easy. Tall and angular, she had straight black hair to her shoulders, milky white skin, and piercing green eyes. The word that immediately came to Daphne's mind was *striking*.

"Hi Sloane. What are you doing here?" Skylar said with a friendly smile. Daphne was impressed by how relaxed she seemed when she was clearly anything but.

Sloane held up a textbook and did not return the smile. "I forgot this the other night. I have an exam on Friday, so Dad left it with Stephen for me to pick up." Despite her beauty, her eyes were cold as she spoke, her face tense.

"I thought you were headed to the Catskills with your friends for the long weekend. Or did I hear that wrong?" Skylar asked with noticeable warmth.

"No, you heard right. We're leaving today. I'm kind of in a hurry, actually. I don't want everyone to wonder where I am." She briefly made eye contact with Daphne and KC but still didn't smile.

"Oh yes, of course. Then I won't keep you. Let me quickly introduce you to my friends. Sloane, meet my nearest and dearest from college, Daphne and KC, also known as the other Musketeers. Daphne and KC, this is Sloane, James's daughter."

KC grinned. "It's great to meet you, Sloane. We hear you go to Columbia?"

Sloane nodded politely.

"She's an *excellent* student. James is always bragging about her grades. So you have a midterm coming up? That makes me think of the marathon cramming sessions we used to have before exams at Northwestern." Skylar looked at Daphne and KC. "Remember those? Remember how much sugar we'd eat to keep us up?"

"I still think about them every time I see Swedish Fish," Daphne said.

"Swedish Fish! I used to love those!" KC said.

"Do you do that with your friends too? Stay up all night studying and eating junk food to stay awake?" Skylar asked Sloane.

Sloane half shrugged but didn't reply.

"It must be so fun going to school in a killer place like New York City," KC said.

Skylar put her hand on KC's head. "KC lives in California. Apparently they still say *killer* there."

Sloane didn't laugh at the joke. "I'd really better get going. My friends are waiting for me." She gave them a chilly half smile, then turned and disappeared around the corner.

When Sloane was well out of earshot, Skylar held her hands out and sighed. "See? She hates me."

KC rubbed Skylar's shoulder. "Ah, don't say that."

"I keep asking her to invite some of her friends over to the apartment for dinner or to study or just to hang out so I can get to know them—and so she can see that I'm not some monster stepmother, you know? But she never has. Not one time. It's like she's embarrassed by me or something."

"She's a college student," Daphne said. "All college students are standoffish."

*Is that even true?* She didn't think so, but she didn't know what else to say at the moment. *Ice Princess is an understatement!*

Skylar's shoulders slumped. "I try to connect with her by asking about her life at school and her friends, and by telling her about myself and my friends when I was her age. Like the way I did just now, with our cram sessions? I keep hoping that sharing stories like that will make me seem more relatable to her, but nothing resonates. Anytime I even bring *up* those days she just looks at me like I'm a fossil, like there's no way my college experience could have been anything remotely like hers. I mean, I'm not *that* old, right?"

"To her you probably are. I remember thinking twenty-five was over the hill when I was a teenager," Daphne said.

Skylar covered her mouth with her hand. "Oh god, you're right. I remember thinking that too. No wonder she looks at me like I'm crazy for reminiscing about the good ol' days. She probably thinks we rode around campus in a horse and buggy!"

KC stomped her foot. "Stop that right now, both of you! We're not *old*, okay? We're just older than she is. And as for the way she acts around you, Skylar, my two cents is that it's probably just a phase, so try not to worry about it. I remember when Max's sons were teenagers and pulled the too-cool-for-school act with us. Both of them did it at some point. It definitely wasn't fun for me and Max, but it was just a phase and didn't last. They're not at all like that now—far from it."

Daphne nodded. "Emma gets like that sometimes too, especially when she thinks I pry too much. I think it's part of growing up. They need to show they don't need you. Plus remember that Sloane's still getting used to having you around. Maybe she feels that her dad is betraying her mom's memory?"

"Could be," Skylar said. "Ugh. I can only imagine what holidays and family vacations are going to be like. How can I compete with a ghost?"

"Just give it time. She'll come around," KC said.

"What does James think?" Daphne asked.

"He's a single dad who works a lot. I think he just figures she's a typical college student and that I'm reading too much into it."

"Maybe," Daphne said. "By the way, isn't Columbia out of session now? Why does she have a midterm?"

"Summer school. Apparently she wants to graduate early, although why anyone would want to enter the real world even one minute faster than necessary is beyond me. I've mentioned that to her, that she should enjoy her college days for as long as possible because they're precious and finite, but it falls upon deaf ears. She's pretty driven and smart as a whip, I'll give her that. On the dean's list every semester."

KC elbowed Skylar. "Sounds like someone I know."

Skylar reached for the lobby door. "Maybe a little."

*Maybe a lot*, Daphne thought.

# Chapter Eleven

"Look! It's the Statue of Liberty! Isn't she beautiful?" KC pointed at the iconic landmark, then stood up from her seat and approached the railing of the ferry.

Skylar elbowed Daphne. "I love how she refers to a statue as a person."

"Only she could make that sound endearing and not weird," Daphne said.

In the background, a jovial tour guide peppered his spiel about the landmarks they were passing with trivia questions about lesser-known New York City geography. Unfortunately, most of them were met with blank stares by tourists who had never been to New York, or who didn't speak English, or both, so Skylar had been interjecting with answers to keep the awkward silence from lingering too long.

Daphne was about to comment on the spectacular view of the Manhattan skyline when Skylar suddenly yelled out "Frank Sinatra!" in response to a question about a New Jersey crooner who hailed from just across the Hudson River. She looked at Daphne, who was trying not to laugh, and lifted her sunglasses. "What? You want me to just let the poor tour guide sit there until some lady from Nebraska looks it up on her phone?"

"Next time just try not to shout in my ear, okay? You sound like KC," Daphne said.

Skylar shrugged and put her sunglasses back on. "Fair enough. It does drive me nuts when she yells for no reason."

Just then, KC returned to the bench.

"Hey you, we were just talking about you." Daphne said.

"Heckling you, if we're being honest," Skylar added.

KC quietly sat down without speaking, one hand on her abdomen.

"You okay there?" Skylar asked.

"I don't feel so hot," KC said. Her skin looked pale and clammy.

"Morning sickness or sea sickness?" Daphne asked.

"I think maybe a combination of both, although I haven't had morning sickness so far and I've never had a problem with boats. But I feel really nauseous."

"Maybe it was all that bacon you ate?" Skylar said.

"You did kind of inhale it," Daphne said.

"Please don't mention bacon right now," KC said.

"You want me to take you to the bathroom?" Daphne asked.

"Yes, please."

The hue of her skin suddenly looked a bit green.

"You want me to come along?" Skylar asked.

"It's fine, I've got her. You can keep the tour guide company." Daphne put an arm around KC and began walking her to the covered area of the boat. As she descended the steps she heard Skylar yell "Governors Island!" She glanced back at Skylar and laughed. Skylar made a *Hey what can you do?* shrug.

When Daphne and KC reached the lower deck, Daphne barely had time to open the bathroom door before KC lurched forward, fell to her knees, and began throwing up into the toilet. Daphne quietly shut the door behind her and stood guard to make sure no one would bother her friend. Fortunately, the bottom level of the ferry was empty, as everyone was up top to enjoy the views.

A few minutes later Daphne heard the toilet flush, then water running in the sink. Soon KC emerged. The color was back in her face but she looked a little weary.

"Sorry about that," she said. "That's never happened to me before."

"Don't apologize. I've been pregnant too, remember? Are you feeling better?"

KC nodded. "Much better. I just hope that doesn't happen again."

"It probably will, just so you know. Kind of comes with the territory."

"Great," KC said.

They made their way back upstairs and saw Skylar standing against the railing, gazing upward as they prepared to pass under the Brooklyn Bridge. KC poked her in the back. "Hey tall person, you're blocking the view."

Skylar turned around and held out her arms. "She's alive!"

"Good as new," Daphne said.

"I just tossed my cookies," KC announced.

Skylar laughed. "The last time I remember you doing that was at the Sigma Chi spring fling. At least Daphne didn't have to hold your ponytail this time." She looked at Daphne. "Or did you?"

"Not this time, although of course I would have if she had needed me to, as that is the truest form of female friendship there is," Daphne said.

Skylar nodded. "Well said."

Just then the tour guide shouted yet another question to the ferry-goers. "Which annual, world-famous event begins at the foot of the Verrazano Bridge, which you can now see in the distance off the starboard, or right, side of the boat?"

"The New York Marathon!" Skylar shouted, and the grateful tour guide gave her a thumbs-up sign.

"You're on fire," Daphne said.

"I do what I can. Did you see all the blank stares the poor guy was getting? And those were from the tourists who are still paying attention. The rest of them are busy giving their selfie sticks a workout."

Daphne surveyed the deck. "There are a frightful number of selfie sticks on this ferry ride."

KC grabbed onto the railing. "On another note, is this thing almost over? I'm going to kiss the ground when we return to dry land."

"Have a seat and try not to think about it, babe. We'll be done before you know it," Skylar said.

KC plopped down on the nearest bench. Daphne pulled a bottle of water from her purse and handed it to her. "Hang in there."

"The Brooklyn Promenade!" Skylar suddenly shouted in the direction of the tour guide.

Daphne laughed and put a hand over Skylar's mouth. "Could you at least give the tourists a *chance* to answer? They paid for this too, you know."

Skylar laughed too. "Okay, fine. Let's talk about something juicy to keep me distracted. Hey what about *your* love life? We've barely talked about that. How are things going with Derek?"

"Good! I mean, so far. We're taking it slow because of the distance."

"Would you ever move to Chicago? You know, if things got serious?" KC asked.

Daphne shook her head. "Not if Emma goes to OSU."

"Why not?" Skylar said.

"Because she might need me close by."

"What for? To do her laundry? Do you *remember* college, Daphne? Parents are persona non grata." Skylar made scissors with her fingers. "Have you ever heard of apron strings?"

"Hey, didn't you make that same gesture last night to describe a vasectomy?" KC said.

Skylar shrugged. "It's a multifunction gesture. The point is, college kids don't want their parents hovering over them."

Daphne wondered if Skylar was right. *Am I soon going to be a persona non grata in my own daughter's life?*

KC poked Skylar's side. "Be nice. You know how much Daphne adores Emma. Max and I went through the empty-nest pain. It's a real thing, even for me as a stepmother relatively new to the scene. When those boys packed up and left for college, both times I put on a brave face, but I'm not gonna lie. Once I shut the front door, I cried like a baby."

"*Your* baby is going to have such a wonderful mommy," Daphne said to KC.

"Aw, thanks, Daph."

Skylar held up her hands in surrender. "You know what? You're right. I'm sorry. Who am I to be talking about apron strings when I've never worn them? You guys see now why I'm going to be a horrible stepmother? No wonder Sloane hates me."

"I'm sure she doesn't hate you, regardless of how she acted back there," Daphne said.

*How could anyone not love Skylar?*

"I agree with Daphne. Who could hate *you?*" KC asked.

"Lots of people. I'm mean at work, remember?"

"I refuse to believe that," KC said. "You could never be mean."

"I agree with KC. Assertive, yes. Mean, never. There's a big difference. Just ask your buddy over there." Daphne waved to the tour guide, who grinned and waved back at them.

•     •     •

"What kind of wedding are you planning to have?" Daphne asked Skylar as they rode the escalator to the seventh floor of Bergdorf's on Fifth Avenue a short while later. "Big? Small? Destination? Local?" She figured it would be expensive, probably outrageously so. With each floor they passed, she eyed the well-heeled patrons browsing brand names she'd never heard of and wondered if it was obvious to them that she had no business shopping in a store like this.

"No idea. Our schedules are both so nuts that we haven't even been able to pick a date, much less a place. James said he'd be happy to get married anywhere, even city hall, but I feel like we should do something more traditional."

"Max and I got married at city hall," KC said.

"That's right! I forgot about that, you sneaky little thing. You didn't even tell us until afterward," Skylar said.

"I still feel bad about that," KC said.

"Don't. I'm just giving you a hard time," Skylar said as she stepped off the escalator. "I know you didn't invite anyone except immediate family."

Daphne looked at the cabinets filled with swanky glassware and silver as they made their way to the wedding dress section. "I think anything you find here is going to be on the fancy side for a city hall wedding." She turned to KC. "Didn't you wear a dress from J. Crew to yours?"

KC grinned. "I still wear it sometimes. How many brides get to say *that?*"

"I would guess one, including you," Daphne said.

"In fact, I brought it this weekend," KC said.

"I take it that's because it's your *only* dress, besides the one we made you buy in Saint Mirika, of course," Skylar said.

"You are correct," KC said. "And I brought that one too."

"Well, wherever I get married and whatever dress I wear, don't worry, I won't make you two be bridesmaids. I refuse to inflict that pain on people I love," Skylar said as they reached the bridal area, which was tucked into a back corner and was much smaller than Daphne had expected, given the size of the store. The dresses on display, however, were breathtaking.

"Being a bridesmaid's not *that* bad," KC said. "I think it's kind of fun."

Skylar arched an eyebrow. "Besides your own, how many weddings have you been in?"

KC held up two fingers. "Daphne's, and my cousin's."

Skylar held up nine fingers. "That's *my* number, and the novelty wore off around number four, maybe even number three. And after all of them I either gave the dress to Goodwill or left it hanging in the closet at the hotel. So there you go. No bridesmaids for me, which means no ugly dresses for you." She made the *safe* signal, like an umpire.

Daphne put a hand on her heart. "Were *my* bridesmaid dresses ugly?"

"Sweets, you got married like twenty years ago. Everything was ugly then," Skylar said.

Daphne laughed. "I can't argue with that."

"Welcome to Bergdorf's. I'm Ellie. May I help you?" a smiling woman said as she approached. She had her blonde hair swept up in a classic twist, wore smart black-framed glasses, and carried a clipboard.

"Yes, I have an appointment. The name's Flanagan."

The woman glanced at the clipboard. "Ah yes, Ms. Flanagan! We've been expecting you. Please, follow me. Would you and your friends care for some champagne?"

Skylar nodded. "Why *yes*, I believe my friends and I *would* care for some champagne. That would be lovely, thank you."

"None for me, please." KC patted her stomach.

"Daphne and I will gladly drink yours, right Daphne? Now come on ladies, let's go pick me out a wedding dress."

•   •   •

Seventeen rejected dresses later, Skylar called out to Daphne and KC from behind the curtain of the dressing room. "Okay ladies, I think maybe this next one is it."

"Are you sure?" Daphne said. "It's not even close to being dark outside yet."

"Your sarcasm is not appreciated," Skylar said.

KC yawned. "I appreciate it. I'm falling asleep here."

"I'm right there with you," Daphne said with a yawn of her own.

A moment later, Skylar emerged and stepped onto the little stage in front of her friends.

Daphne caught her breath. "Wow."

"That one's beautiful, Skylar," KC said.

The floor-length gown was an ivory silk taffeta, fitted A-line with a V-neck and delicate beading. The train was not too long but trailed just enough, Daphne thought. Just like Skylar, the dress was elegant and classy but not the least bit stuffy.

"You like?" Skylar said.

"I *love*," KC said.

"Me too." Daphne set down her glass and stood up, suddenly feeling the effects of multiple glasses of champagne. "It's gorgeous, Skylar. You look stunning."

"It's like it was meant for you," KC said. "I don't think I've ever seen you look so beautiful."

Daphne approached the stage. "Can I touch it?"

Skylar laughed. "Of course you can. It's a dress, not a rattlesnake."

Daphne stepped up onto the stage and circled Skylar, her walk a bit unsteady. As she finished the loop she noticed a tiny price tag attached to the dress. She leaned down and squinted, then audibly gasped when she saw the number on it.

Skylar turned and gave her a strange look. "Everything okay?"

Daphne carefully stepped down. "Yep, all good. Will you excuse me for a minute? I'm going to use the ladies' room."

On the way to the restroom, Daphne looked at the various china patterns on display, each one more expensive than the next. She wondered if Skylar and James would bother registering, given that they probably already had everything they needed. She remembered having picked out china with Brian so long ago and felt a pang of sadness. She'd been so full of hope on her own wedding day, but then things had turned out so differently from how she'd expected.

*What was it that Krissa had said earlier in her big speech about dating? Something about how we'll drive ourselves crazy if we try to figure out love?*

Daphne *had* been in love with Brian, even though it hadn't worked out for the long haul.

*Could Cupid really strike twice for me?*

For a moment she thought of Derek, but then suddenly her thoughts turned to Clay and how she'd reacted when she'd seen him—or thought she'd seen him. She enjoyed Derek's company, but he had never affected her pulse like that. She still had Clay's number in her phone.

*Maybe I should reach out to him to say hi? There's no harm in that, right?*

She remembered how much fun she'd had with him during the brief time they'd spent together in Saint Mirika, and how good he'd made her feel about herself during a very difficult time in her life. For that, she'd always be grateful to him.

Emboldened by the champagne, she tapped out a text.

*Hi Clay, it's Daphne from Saint Mirika. How are you? I know it's been ages, but you said to get in touch if I ever came to New York. Well, guess what? I'm here! Would love to catch up if you're around.*

She checked over the note for typos, then clicked "Send." She decided not to tell Skylar or KC what she'd done. That way if he didn't respond, they would never have to know about it. She also felt a little guilty.

*What would Derek think?*

When Daphne returned to the changing area, Skylar still had the dress on and was standing in front of the mirror.

"I love it, Skylar," KC said. "I think that's the one."

"Me too. I have no idea where or even when I'm going to wear it, but I'm going to get it."

"Well, wherever and whenever that is, you're going to *rock* it," KC said.

"You really do look incredible, Skylar," Daphne said with a sudden hiccup.

Skylar turned around and laughed. "Did you just hiccup?"

Daphne pointed to the champagne bottle. "I blame the bubbly."

Skylar clapped her hands twice and stepped off the stage. "Okay ladies, now that finding a dress is checked off the agenda, it's time for lunch at the Boathouse, one of my favorite spots in the city. We can walk there, which will give Buzzy McBuzzerson here a chance to sober up."

Daphne hiccupped again. "I like that plan."

# Chapter Twelve

"The restaurant we're going to is actually *in* the park?" Daphne asked as they crossed Central Park South and left the city streets behind.

"Yep, the Boathouse is another Manhattan treasure. I hope you two are hungry again. The lobster rolls there are delicious," Skylar said.

"I'm always hungry these days," KC said.

The myriad pathways traversing Central Park were bustling with New Yorkers and tourists alike, everyone out for a Saturday stroll on the magical, tree-lined walkways of one of the most beautiful playgrounds in the world. The grassy areas were dotted with picnic dwellers and sunbathers, their relative stillness contrasted by the movement of kite flyers, hula-hoopers, and freestyling acrobats sprinkled about. Also in constant motion were swarms of happy children running through and around weekend warriors tossing or kicking footballs, Frisbees, baseballs, and soccer balls. The free-flowing scene played out to an eclectic soundtrack provided by various guitar, flute, and saxophone players, as well as the steady beat of drum circles scattered here and there. Yet despite the large numbers the park didn't appear overcrowded, as there were enough nooks and crannies to absorb everyone.

Daphne, Skylar, and KC walked along in comfortable silence for a few minutes, each taking in the sights and sounds in her own way. As they passed an ice cream cart, the third she'd seen since entering the park, Daphne spoke up. "All these ice cream vendors remind me of something funny my neighbor Carol once told me. Her kids are grown now, but she said that when they were little, she taught them that when the ice cream truck drove through our neighborhood playing music, it meant it was *out* of ice cream."

"That's so sneaky!" KC said.

"Isn't it? She said her kids were super mad at her when they finally figured it out, but they use it on their own kids now," Daphne said.

"It's genius," Skylar said. "Think how much she must have saved not just in the cost of ice cream, but in dental bills."

Soon they approached the Boathouse entrance. "We have a reservation, but there might still be a wait given how nice the weather is today—no one will want to leave! If so, we can always get a drink at the bar, although I may have to cut this one off." Skylar gestured to Daphne.

Daphne held up a finger. "For the record, I think I'm completely sober now. Almost."

KC spotted a couple pushing a stroller to the left side of the entrance. The woman looked to be in her mid-forties, the man a few years older. "Hey, look at them! They look just like me and Max will be in a few months. You think I should go say hi?"

Skylar shrugged. "Why not? They're your people now. Go make nice and request your membership card, or whatever official form of ID the club provides. Daphne and I will go check on our table."

KC gave them the thumbs-up sign. "Coolio. See you inside."

•    •    •

"I'm officially stuffed," Daphne said as she set her fork down next to a half-eaten lobster roll and leaned back against her chair. "That was delicious, but I can't eat another bite."

"If you're not going to finish that, can I have it?" KC asked. "I'm eating for two, you know."

"It's all yours." Daphne set her plate in front of KC, then turned to watch the smattering of rowboats slowly gliding across the lake just outside the floor-to-ceiling windows of the Boathouse. Like so much of the scenery she'd seen so far this weekend, the setting seemed straight out of a movie.

"So when do we get those presents you were talking about earlier?" Skylar asked KC. "I've been waiting all day."

"Ah yes! The presents!" Daphne looked at KC. "I love presents."

"Oops! I totally forgot. I meant to give them to you guys at the bridal salon. My bad." KC reached into her purse for the pink gift bag, then pulled out two small, giftwrapped boxes. She handed one to Daphne and one to Skylar. "A special gift for two very special people."

Daphne and Skylar unwrapped their boxes. Inside of each, on a bed of cotton, lay a bracelet. The simple design was composed of a ring of clear beads, with a single white bead and a single black bead at opposite ends of the circle.

"I like it," Skylar said as she lifted the bracelet.

KC grinned. "Isn't it groovy? It's called a Lokai bracelet. They're all the rage in Southern California."

"A low what?" Daphne said as she tried it on.

"A Lokai. I got myself one too." KC reached into the bag and pulled out one more bracelet, then slipped it onto her wrist and held it up under the hanging light. "It's made of elements from the highest and lowest points on earth." She touched the black bead on one side. "This little guy here is filled with mud from the Dead Sea." Then she moved her finger to the white bead. "And this one is filled with water from Mount Everest."

Daphne squinted at her bracelet. "There's really mud and water in there? From those actual places?"

"Yep. Isn't that neat? They say it's to represent the emotional peaks and valleys in our lives." KC fingered the beads again, then tapped the black one with her index finger. "The Dead Sea mud symbolizes those times when you're really down in the dumps, when it seems like nothing is going your way and the universe seems to be conspiring against you."

Daphne nodded. "I'm a little familiar with that feeling. Remember what a wreck I was when I found out Brian was getting remarried?" She didn't want to let on that she was beginning to feel low about herself again lately.

*There's still one more agent. Stay positive!*

"I've felt like that too," KC said, then pointed at Daphne, then at Skylar. "And before you two give me a look of disbelief, *yes*, even we overly cheerful types have our moments when we'd rather stay under the covers than get out of bed and face the day. And I'm not talking about the *fun times* under the covers. I'm a big fan of those." She giggled.

Skylar pointed to KC's belly. "Apparently so."

KC touched the black bead again, then continued. "Anyhow, this guy here reminds us to have *hope* during those valleys, to remember that gloom and doom won't last forever." She rotated the bracelet until the white bead was at the top, then gently tapped it a few times. "The water from Mount Everest symbolizes those magical times when everything is clicking for you, when you're on top of the world, when life feels amazing and you wouldn't want to change a single thing." She raised her hand high in the air to let the bracelet catch the sunlight. "Aren't those times the best? When you're on a natural high?"

"Call me a capitalist, but I feel like that every time I sign a new account," Skylar said.

*Skylar has clearly signed a lot of accounts,* Daphne thought.

KC began running her fingers over the row of clear beads in between the black and white ones. "Now, I love the highs and dread the lows, but when I really think about it, *these* little boys are my favorites."

"What do they represent?" Skylar asked.

"You know that saying, 'Life is what happens when you're busy making other plans'?" She twisted her wrist back and forth. "Well, that's who these guys are, the times *in between* the emotional highs and lows that take so much of our energy. They're the behind-the-scenes nitty-gritty that makes up everyday life when we're not paying attention. They're clear to remind us to *pay attention*, to *keep moving*, to remember that e*very moment in our lives is important*, no matter how uneventful it may seem at the time. And you know what else the clear beads do? They remind us that nothing lasts forever, no matter how much it hurts or how good it feels. In times of both sadness *and* joy, clarity is useful." She gave the bracelet one more pat. "So there you have it in a nutshell, albeit a long-winded nutshell. The Lokai bracelet is comprised of the good, the bad, and the in-between. Together the three elements represent the journey of life—and encourage us to enjoy the ride with our eyes and hearts open. I hope all that didn't sound too flower child for you guys. I know I can be a little out there sometimes."

"Not at all," Daphne said. "I think what you said was quite … profound."

Skylar nodded. "Very Zen."

KC grinned. "*Profound* and *Zen*. I like that description. I'll have to remember that the next time Max calls me a hippie space cadet."

# Chapter Thirteen

When the taxi pulled up in front of Skylar's building after lunch, Daphne blocked Skylar with her arm and quickly swiped her credit card in the backseat mechanism. "You have to let us pay for *something*," she said. Skylar had picked up the tab for brunch and lunch, as well as the ferry ride.

Skylar shrugged. "Okay, fine. But if you try that move at dinner tonight, that arm of yours is going to end up in a sling."

"Where are we eating?" KC asked as they climbed out of the car.

"You can't possibly be hungry *again*," Skylar said.

"Nah, just curious about the restaurant," KC said. "But I'll definitely be ready to eat by then. And now that I think about it, I'll probably be up for a little snack before then too."

"I remember feeling starved all the time when I was pregnant with Emma," Daphne said. "There were days when I'd have three peanut butter, butter, and lettuce sandwiches before ten in the morning."

"Good lord! How much did she weigh when she was born?" Skylar asked. "That combination sounds disgusting, by the way."

Daphne laughed. "I know, but I craved those things like you wouldn't believe. And yes, Emma was a little chunky as a baby, but cute chunky."

"I love chunky babies," KC said. "They remind me of those little roly-poly bugs,"

"Okay, Emma was actually pretty chubby when she was little. We used to call her 'the tank.' Then she hit kindergarten and turned into a beanpole almost overnight," Daphne said.

"If you could figure out how to replicate that for adults, you'd make a fortune," Skylar said.

After they stepped from the elevator into the apartment, KC yawned and made a beeline for a couch in the living room. "Well, I don't know about you two, but I'm exhausted. Anyone down for a nap?"

Skylar yawned too and sat on the couch next to KC. "That sounds like a fabulous idea. Playing tourist combined with trying on wedding dresses is exhausting."

"Should we all crash in the same bed?" KC asked. "Remember when we used to do that in college?"

"We used to do a lot of things in college that I would never do again," Skylar said. "I love you to death, but I'm not taking a nap with you."

KC crossed her arms in front of her and pretended to look upset. "Okay, fine. Have it your way. What about you, Daph? You in the mood for an afternoon snooze?"

Daphne shook her head. "I think I'll do a little window-shopping and see if I can pick up something for Emma. Seems like there are a lot of cute stores around here."

*Expensive stores,* she imagined. *Maybe I'll get lucky and find something on sale.*

"When you get out of the building, head north toward SoHo. There's a ton of great shopping there. Stephen can point you in the right direction," Skylar said to Daphne.

"Thanks. Do you have a hat I can borrow? I feel like I've had enough sun."

"Sure thing. I have a bunch in my closet. You can have your pick."

The three of them headed downstairs, and when they reached KC's room she yawned again. "Naptime for me and the baby. I'll see you two beauties when I wake up." She turned and padded inside.

Daphne followed Skylar into the master suite, which she had yet to see as they'd forgotten all about the grand tour Skylar had been meaning to give. She felt her eyes expand at the enormity of the bedroom. It was twice the size of Daphne's living room and appeared even larger due to the high ceilings. White carpeting and pale blue walls gave the room a cool-yet-inviting vibe, and there was a king sleigh bed to the left paired with a comfy white couch, ottoman and recliner chair to the right. An enormous flat-screen TV was mounted on the wall next to a brick fireplace. Everything looked brand-new and posh, but like the living room and the guest room Daphne was staying in, there were no artwork, candles, picture frames, or decorative accents of any kind.

Daphne admired the furniture, which didn't seem to include a dresser—at least a visible one. Then she realized why.

"The closet's back here," Skylar said as they passed the bathroom, which was three—if not four—times the size of Daphne's, from what she could tell by a quick peek. Beyond that was a door-less frame leading to the largest walk-in closet Daphne had ever seen. When they entered it, she immediately noticed a sizeable chandelier hanging from the ceiling.

*A chandelier? In a closet?*

"This closet is bigger than my entire bedroom, Skylar," she said.

Skylar shrugged. "I know it's a little much, but what can I say? I have a lot of clothes. Although James does too, so I'm not *entirely* to blame. She pointed to the rear of the room. Hats are over there."

"Which one should I wear?" Daphne spotted at least ten. And that was just summer hats. White, blue, yellow, striped—all in a variety of styles and materials.

"Any one you like, sweets. What's mine is yours. I'm going to give James a quick call before I take a nap, so I'll leave you to it."

"Okay, thanks." Daphne stood there for a moment after Skylar was gone, wondering what it would be like to have a closet like this, to have a wardrobe like this, to have a *life* like this. She noticed a sturdy, full-length mirror standing in a roomy corner and thought of the flimsy mirror on the back of her own bedroom door, which she'd hung there herself in an effort to maximize space. She took a step toward the dress area and ran a hand along the beautiful assortment of expensive fabrics and designs, then did the same with the tops— a colorful variety of blouses mixed with more casual wear—and bottoms, which included jeans, pants, and skirts. Another wall was filled entirely with tailored business suits.

Then she saw the shoe racks, lined with pair upon pair of assorted pumps, stiletto heels, strappy heels, kitten heels, ballerina flats, knee-high boots, ankle boots, wedges, sneakers, sandals, and flip-flops—row after row of meticulously displayed designer footwear. It was a far cry from the tangled heap on the floor of her own small closet.

Daphne sighed. *Being here is like shopping in a department store. An extremely upscale one.*

She glanced in the mirror at the sundress she had on and wondered if it was obvious that she'd bought it at TJ Maxx.

*Does it look "last season?"*

She'd gotten so used to shopping at discount stores that she never paid attention to that sort of thing but wondered if maybe Skylar did.

On top of a large bureau tucked in the far left corner of the closet, in between two jewelry trees draped in earrings, necklaces, and bracelets, she noticed a framed photo of Skylar and James. They were sitting alone at a picnic table in what looked to be a garden, or maybe a well-manicured backyard. In the image they were both laughing, eyes locked on each other, not the camera. Skylar looked to be on the verge of tears—joyful ones. Daphne picked up the frame and studied the image of her friend, whom she'd known for nearly twenty-five years.

*Have I ever seen Skylar look that happy?*

She wasn't sure.

She set down the photo and wandered to the other side of the closet to pick out a hat. After scanning the options she selected a white, floppy one and placed it on her head, then took a step in front of the mirror, cocking her head to one side in surprise at how well the hat complemented her blue dress and added a bit of flair to her outfit. With a tiny smile, she did a few twirls in front of the mirror, liking her stylish new look.

When she returned upstairs, Skylar was on the couch with her legs resting on an ottoman, chatting on her phone. Still wearing the hat, Daphne approached and made a *What do you think?* gesture. Skylar gave a thumbs-up, then covered the phone and mouthed the words, "Love it."

Daphne mouthed the word "shopping," then pointed to the elevator and quietly headed out.

• • •

Knowing her budget most likely couldn't afford the clothes sold in such an exclusive neighborhood, Daphne didn't really plan to do more than window-shop. But she always enjoyed a good walk and was looking forward to exploring more of Tribeca and the surrounding area. From what she'd seen of Manhattan so far, the city seemed to transform itself every few blocks, both in architecture and character, something she found immensely appealing.

*What neighborhood would I have called home if I'd moved here after college? Would I have ended up in a cozy brownstone or a modern high-rise?*

After wandering up and down West Broadway for a bit, then through the winding cobblestone streets of the Financial District, she headed north again toward Tribeca. She was steps away from a boutique whose pretty window dressing had caught her eye when she noticed a small bookshop next door. She stopped and gazed longingly at the book jackets displayed front and center, wondering what it would feel like to see her own work there, her *own name* on the spine of a book. She looked down at her purse and wondered if she should check her e-mail again. There was still one agent left.

*Maybe there's a message right now in my in-box? Maybe all those NO replies have set me up for the one and only YES I need.*

She knew she should wait until she got back to Columbus to check, but before she knew it she was fumbling for her phone. She scrolled through the new messages and caught her breath when she saw it: A message from the last remaining literary agent.

*Oh my God!*

She closed her eyes and said a quick prayer to the universe, then clicked to open the e-mail.

*Dear Daphne,*
*Thank you for submitting your manuscript, which I enjoyed immensely. It is well written, poignant at times, and fun. Unfortunately, however, I just don't see a place for it on my list, so I will be unable to offer you representation at this time. I wish you the best of luck in finding a home for your lovely story.*
*Best,*
*AP*

Daphne had barely finished reading the message before she felt tears begin to sting her eyes.

*Well written and fun, but no thanks? What am I supposed to make of that?*

A crushing weight descended upon her as the optimism she'd been trying so hard to hold on to instantly dissolved. For more than a year, she'd dedicated countless hours to creating a story that had—at least according to this agent—multiple positive attributes. She'd poured her heart and soul into it and flourished as she did so, editing and rewriting for months on end until she had something she *knew* was good.

*And for what? To feel like a complete and utter failure? Could I really be such a bad writer that not* one *agent will take me on?*

Writing was the one thing at which she'd actually believed she was talented, the one thing that made her feel like more than just an ex-wife relying on alimony payments, child support, and a low-paying part-time job.

*But what was the point if all it's led to is an overwhelming sense of disappointment?*

She looked up and saw her reflection in the bookstore window, suddenly feeling foolish in Skylar's fancy hat.

*Who am I trying to kid? I'm not talented or special, or on the verge of being discovered. I'm just a drab, wannabe writer from Ohio.*

She dabbed her eyes with a tissue and tried not to look at the books in the display, a place her own manuscript would apparently never call home.

"I love your hat," a woman suddenly said to Daphne as she passed by. "Very chic."

Daphne blinked in surprise. "Oh, thank you."

She watched the woman walk away, then, almost without realizing what she was doing, turned and entered the boutique adjacent to the bookstore.

A smiling young shopkeeper approached. "Good afternoon. Looking for anything in particular today?"

Daphne nodded. "A makeover."

•  •  •

"There you are. Where have you been? We were about to put out an APB," Skylar said when Daphne returned to the apartment.

"Sorry, I lost track of time. I went on a little shopping spree." Daphne joined Skylar and KC in the living room, several large shopping bags in tow.

Skylar eyed the bags. "*Little?* I know you're the words person, but *little* doesn't seem like quite the right adjective given all this loot."

KC whistled. "Look at you. You're in New York for one day and suddenly you're Julia Roberts in *Pretty Woman*—minus the being a hooker part, of course."

Daphne set down the bags and removed Skylar's hat as she took a seat on the couch. "You weren't kidding when you said there was good shopping around here. Once I got started I couldn't stop myself."

"What did you get? Apparently a new wardrobe and then some," Skylar said.

Daphne pointed at the bags one by one. "A few dresses, some tops, jeans and skirts, a jacket, a couple sweaters, a few pairs of shoes, some jewelry."

*And all of it too expensive for my budget.*

As she listed the items—*categories* of items—out loud, the magnitude of what she'd spent in the blink of an eye began to sink in.

*Why? What has gotten into me? Have I lost my mind?*

The bags in front of her held more new things than she'd bought for herself in years.

"Nothing wrong with indulging in a shopping spree while on vacation," Skylar said. "And what better timing, given all the signings and interviews you're going to have to do when your novel comes out? I bet they'll send you on a coast-to-coast book tour."

"I can't wait to go to a book signing in California and brag about how I'm *with the author* as I push my way past the line of rabid fans clamoring for an autograph," KC said.

Daphne stared at the pile of merchandise and felt her neck get hot.

*How can I tell them the truth now?*

"Will you model the loot for us?" Skylar asked.

"Can it wait? I'm kind of beat," Daphne said, feeling sicker by the minute over what she'd done. She imagined what a binge eater must feel like and felt a rush of shame for having lost control like that.

Skylar checked her watch, then stood up. "Actually, holding the fashion show over until tomorrow is probably a good idea anyway, given how late it's getting. We've really got to get a move on or we're going to miss our dinner reservation, and this is one reservation you do *not* want to miss. Chop chop, ladies."

*Saved by the dinner bell,* Daphne thought.

# Chapter Fourteen

"Holy moly, Skylar!" KC craned her neck at the sparkling circular chandeliers and ornate ceiling carvings as the hostess led them to their table at Daniel, an Upper East Side French/American restaurant with a tasting menu—and two Michelin stars. Daphne had never been to a place with either.

While KC fixated on the high ceilings, Daphne's eyes were drawn to the soaring arches and rows of white pillars that separated the grandiose room into intimate-yet-open dining spaces. "Holy moly is right. This is like something out of a James Bond movie," she said.

"Isn't it? A client brought me here once years ago, and I've been wanting to come back ever since," Skylar said.

"I'm glad I brought my *wedding dress* this weekend, otherwise I'd have nothing to wear to a restaurant this fancy," KC said as she poked Skylar's side.

Skylar, the embodiment of style in a sleeveless green dress perfectly tailored to her figure, poked KC back. "I'm just glad you're not wearing a baseball hat! But you do look great." She turned to Daphne. "You look lovely too, by the way. That color really suits you."

"Thanks. That's what the saleslady said too."

Daphne looked down at her new dress, a light pink cap-sleeve sheath, and felt another rush of buyer's remorse. The dress was one of the cheaper—or better said, *less* expensive—items she'd purchased earlier, but she still felt terribly guilty over what she'd spent. She'd already decided to sneak out and take everything back tomorrow, with the exception of what she currently had on, of course. She could justify buying *one* new dress on her New York trip. She hoped Skylar would forget about the fashion show idea, although she knew the chances of that were probably slim. Skylar never forgot anything.

•   •   •

The tasting menu was comprised of a number of tiny plates, the presentation of each course seemingly more elaborate than the last. Each was served as if the diners were royalty: foie gras mosaic rutabaga, birch-poached Asian pear with burgundy truffle vinaigrette, key-lime marinated fluke, sea urchin, white sturgeon caviar, anise hyssop salad, sunchoke confit. Just to name a few. On and on it went, and while KC and Skylar seemed to be having a ball and savoring every bite, to Daphne the cumulative effect of the exquisite cuisine and world-class service was a feeling of unease and self-conscious-ness that continued to grow with each course. She was out of her league here—socially and financially. She had no doubt that Skylar would graciously pick up what had to be a hefty bill, but that only made her feel worse.

When they were finally done with the last dessert plate, KC leaned back in her chair and groaned. "That was the best meal I've ever had, but I may never eat again. I am absolutely stuffed!"

Skylar rolled her eyes. "Give me a break. You're going to walk into the kitchen tomorrow morning whining about being famished. You have the metabolism of a hamster."

KC grinned. "Okay, maybe you're right. I'm definitely falling into a food coma tonight, though. I may even crash in the cab on the way home."

"Please don't tell me you're getting sleepy. I was hoping we could go dancing in the Meatpacking District. There's this new club there with a slide that I've been dying to check out," Skylar said.

Daphne and KC both looked at her, wide-eyed.

"Yes, that was a joke," Skylar said.

"Oh thank God," KC said.

"Shall we hit it?" Skylar pushed her chair back and began to stand up. "And if I haven't made it clear before, your money's no good here. The bill's long been taken care of."

"Thanks Skylar. You're so generous," KC said.

"Yes, thank you, Skylar," Daphne said with a hint of pique in her voice.

• • •

After they left the restaurant, the trio began walking west on Sixty-Fifth toward Central Park. "This neighborhood is so pretty. I just *love* all the brownstones. You said it's called the Upper East Side?" KC asked.

Skylar pointed straight ahead. "Yes, ma'am. If we were to keep walking this way and continue on through the park, which is due west of us, we'd end up on the Upper *West* Side. Hey, that gives me an idea. Before we head back to my place, how about we do just that? We can stop by the Mandarin Oriental at Columbus Circle for a nightcap, my treat. The view of the park from there is spectacular. It's a hotel, but my company had an event in the bar once."

KC raised her hand. "I'm in, although not for a cocktail."

"We'll get you a mocktail," Skylar said.

"A what?" KC said.

Skylar snapped her fingers. "A mock cocktail. Try to keep up, honey."

KC grinned. "Sorry, I'm not hip like you."

*No one is*, Daphne thought.

As if reading Daphne's thoughts, Skylar turned to look at her. "You okay? You're awfully quiet."

Daphne forced a smile. "Just a little tired."

• • •

"To the bride!" KC raised her virgin daiquiri in a toast.

"To the bride." Daphne raised her wine glass but notably didn't demonstrate the same enthusiasm. Now that Skylar had found true love to go with all her other accomplishments, her life—in Daphne's eyes—was officially perfect, quite the contrary to Daphne's own.

Skylar clinked her glass against the others. "Thanks ladies. I'd like to make a toast as well. To good friends getting better with age. I'm getting married, KC's with child, and Daphne's embarking on a literary career—all in our forties! I guess life is full of surprises."

"Life is *definitely* full of surprises." KC patted her stomach.

Skylar set down her glass. "And speaking of surprises, I have a big one for you two. Tomorrow evening, after a visit to my favorite spa to relax, the three of us are heading to the Theater District to see …" She smiled. *"Hamilton!"*

"Oh my God!" KC yelled, then covered her mouth with her hand. "Sorry, I really need to learn to use my inside voice."

"We're in a crowded bar now, so it's fine," Skylar said. "But I appreciate that you're demonstrating growth."

"*Hamilton* as in the hottest show on Broadway?" Daphne said.

"The one and only. You'll love it. I've seen it twice already."

"Of course you have," Daphne muttered under her breath.

Skylar gave her a strange look. "Did you say something?"

"Nope." Daphne buried her nose in her wine glass.

KC took a sip of her mocktail. "This is so exciting. Even Max has said he wants to see *Hamilton*, and he's not a musical kind of guy. He won't even watch a movie if there's not at least one car chase or explosion in it."

Skylar laughed. "The seats I got are *really* good, third row center. Nothing but the best for my inner circle."

"Of course they're good seats," Daphne said, this time not as quietly.

"What did you say?" Skylar asked.

Daphne hesitated, then answered. "I said of *course* they're good seats."

"Are you okay?" Skylar gave her another strange look.

"I told you. I'm tired," said Daphne.

"You don't seem tired," Skylar said. "You seem annoyed."

Daphne finished her wine, then sighed and set down the glass. "Actually, I'm annoyed *and* tired. The truth is, I'm *tired* of the way you keep flaunting your wealth. We get it, okay? You're fabulously successful, your apartment is incredible, your fiancé is perfect, you're so rich that you can buy a wedding dress that costs more than I make in a *year*, and God forbid you stoop so low as to take the subway with the common people. Your life is amazing. Message received. You win."

Skylar's face went pale. Without responding, she stood up and walked away from the table.

Daphne was immediately sickened by the hurtful words she'd just uttered.

*What have I done? How could I have behaved like that?*

She looked at KC, who was staring at her, mouth half-open.

"Why would you say something like that, Daphne?"

Daphne covered her mouth with her hand. "I don't know. I can't believe I just did that. I have to apologize."

She turned her head in the direction Skylar had gone but didn't see her through the crowd. Tears began welling up in her eyes.

*Could I really be the person who just said such horrible things? What is wrong with me?*

She began to feel light-headed. She knew that what she'd done was unforgiveable.

*Skylar will never look at me the same way again. How* could *she?*

"I can't believe I just did that," Daphne said again as she stood up and reached for her purse. "I have to go after her. I have to tell her how sorry I am. I have to see if there's any way she can ever forgive me."

"I'll get the check." KC stood up too and gestured to the waiter.

# Chapter Fifteen

"There she is." KC pointed across Columbus Circle to the southwest entrance of the park. Skylar was sitting alone on a bench as people flowed by in both directions.

"You want me to give you two some space?" KC asked Daphne.

Daphne reached for KC's arm. "No." Together they crossed the busy street, and then Daphne tentatively approached the bench, KC trailing a little behind her. Daphne sat down on one side of Skylar, KC the other.

"Skylar, I lost my mind in there," Daphne said, tears again welling in her eyes. "I don't know why I said those nasty things to you, and you have no idea how sick I feel about it. Please, please try to forgive me. I'm so incredibly sorry."

Skylar stared straight ahead for a few moments, then turned to face her with a pained look that Daphne had never seen. "Do you really feel that way about me? Do you really think I'm trying to … beat you? That I'm a … snob?"

Tears begin to slide down Daphne's cheeks. "*No*, Skylar. You're the most generous person I've ever met. You're smart and talented and loyal and *kind*, and you've worked your tail off to get where you are. You deserve everything you have—*everything.* You're wonderful, and I hope Emma grows up to be just like you."

Skylar began crying too. "Then why would you say those things to me?"

Daphne looked at her hands. She had never seen Skylar cry before. "I think … I think … I'm jealous," she said in a voice so quiet it was almost a whisper. "Seeing your life up close this weekend, your career, your success, everything you have, it makes me feel like I don't … measure up."

"Measure up? What are you talking about, Daphne? We're *friends.* This isn't a competition." Skylar looked at KC. "Do you feel this way too?"

KC quickly shook her head, clearly eager to stay out of the conversation.

Skylar turned back to Daphne. "How can you even compare our lives? That's like comparing apples and television sets. Yes, we chose different paths, but that was a decision, not an indication of intelligence or ability."

"I'm not so sure about that anymore," Daphne said.

"Stop it. I went to school with you for four years, remember? Don't you think I know how bright you are? How *talented* you are? You could have had a huge career if you wanted it."

Daphne felt more tears streaming down her cheeks. "I'm not talented."

"Of course you are. Why would you even say something like that? Remember what a star you were becoming at that magazine before you got married? Those awards you won? And look at what you've done now, even after *years* away from writing. You authored a *book*, Daphne. And it's *good*. Do you know how many people *dream* of doing something like that? Of being *able* to do something like that?"

Daphne shook her head. "It's not going to get published."

"You don't know that," Skylar said.

"I do know it, actually."

"What do you mean?" KC squeaked.

Daphne hesitated for a moment, then decided it was time to share the truth. "I sent the manuscript to three dozen literary agents, and they all passed. *Three dozen*, and every single one said no."

"What?" Skylar said.

Daphne frowned. "All of them. They all turned it down."

"I don't believe that," Skylar said.

"It's true."

"When?" Skylar asked. "When we talked last month you were so jazzed about the whole thing."

Daphne reached for a stick on the ground and began breaking it into pieces. "I was, but then about two weeks ago the rejections started rolling in, and they haven't stopped. It's been a steady stream—no, *flood*—of them filling up my in-box. Yesterday, last night, even today. The last holdout said 'Thanks, but no thanks' just a few hours ago, right before I went temporarily insane and filled five shopping bags with clothes I can't afford, including this dress."

"You've been getting rejections on this trip? Right in front of us? Why didn't you say anything?" Skylar said.

Daphne choked out a laugh. "I was too busy maxing out my credit card in some twisted episode of retail therapy. I was too *embarrassed* to tell you, Skylar. That's what I'm trying to explain. For years, I made myself believe that even though I wasn't actually writing anything, I was a good writer. That if I really wanted to apply myself, I could make a living that way. But it looks like I was deluding myself. That in reality I can't make a living writing, or doing *anything* for that matter. You're getting married, and KC's having a baby, and I'm doing … nothing."

"Oh Daphne, don't be embarrassed. And for the record you're *not* doing nothing. But I'm so sorry about the agents," Skylar said.

Daphne pressed a palm against her eyes. "Please don't apologize. You're only making me feel worse. For nearly twenty-five years you've been nothing but kind to me, and look how I just treated you in return. I'm a terrible friend. I'm a terrible person."

"Stop that. You're a wonderful friend *and* a wonderful person. You're just going through a rough time. That happens to all of us."

Daphne wiped away a tear. "I don't deserve to have you as a friend, Skylar. I'm so sorry for acting like such a psychopath."

"In my opinion, being able to act like a psychopath once in a while is one of the main reasons to *have* friends," Skylar said. "People do crazy things sometimes. It doesn't mean they're actually crazy. And hey, don't forget how much you enjoyed writing that book— regardless of what happens to it."

KC nodded. "You *love* to write, right? And no, using the whatever-you-call-those words that sound the same was not intentional."

"Homonyms. And it's true, I *do* love to write. I need to remember that."

"Telling that story brought joy into your life, Daphne. So published or not and paycheck be damned, you were *not* sitting around doing nothing for the past year. Period," Skylar said.

"Thank you that. I still feel sick about those awful things I said to you. Are you sure you don't hate me?"

"Stop it. I could never hate you. You're family to me. Come here." She pulled Daphne in for a hug, which Daphne eagerly returned. Neither of them said a word, but their embrace expressed as much—if not more—than any words could. As they held each other tight, KC stood up behind them and gently rubbed their backs in silence.

# Chapter Sixteen

The next morning Daphne padded into the kitchen, still in her pajamas. "Morning, bride-to-be," she said with a sleepy yawn to Skylar, who was sitting on a stool at the island, typing furiously on her laptop's keyboard.

"Morning! Can I interest you in a caffeinated beverage?" Skylar pointed to the coffee pot without looking up from her screen.

"You don't have to ask me twice. I assume you're doing something work related?" She hadn't seen Skylar work all weekend but suspected she'd been squeezing it in here and there behind the scenes. It would be decidedly un-Skylar-like to go more than a day without checking on at least one report, client, conference call—or all of the above.

Skylar closed her laptop as Daphne poured herself a cup. "Just a quick update on a call I have next week with APAC. All done now."

"APAC?"

"It's short for Asia Pacific."

"I knew that. Sort of. How do you manage that kind of call with the time difference?" Daphne asked, taking a seat.

"We schedule them after seven."

"After seven p.m.?"

"Yep."

"How often?"

"Depends. A couple, three times a week maybe?"

"You have calls at night multiple times a week?"

Skylar nodded again.

"I guess that's why they pay you the big bucks. Is KC up yet?"

"Haven't seen her. Maybe the baby needs more sleep than she does. What about you? Did you sleep okay?"

"Better than I should have, given how I acted last night. I'm still so sorry for losing it on you like that. I don't know what got into me."

"It's water under the bridge, okay? Please don't beat yourself up about it. Life gets us *all* down now and then—trust me."

Just then KC wandered into the kitchen wearing her pajamas.

"Isn't that right, sunshine? Even you bubbly types have your tough moments, isn't that what you said when you gave us these lovely bracelets?" Skylar held up her wrist.

"I guess so." KC seemed distracted as she climbed onto a stool next to Daphne.

"KC, babe? You okay there?" Skylar waved a hand in front of her.

"Not really," KC said quietly. "I had a dream last night that I kept dropping my baby. I literally couldn't keep hold of her, no matter how hard I tried."

"So? It was a *dream*. I'm pretty sure you're not going to be dropping anyone in real life," Skylar said.

"I bet every mother or expectant mother has dreams like that. I know I sure did," Daphne said. "I wouldn't worry about it. In real life the only place you'll be dropping that baby is off at day care."

Skylar laughed, but KC didn't.

"The truth is … I'm scared," she said quietly.

"Scared about what?" Skylar said.

"I'm scared that I can't … do this."

"Do what?" Daphne asked.

KC put a hand on her belly.

"Oh hon, don't be scared. You'll be a great mom to your little future Olympian. Granted, I've heard the actual *giving birth* part hurts like hell, but you're an athlete. Since when are you afraid of a little bit of pain? What do athletes say, 'No pain no gain'? I bet you have a T-shirt or a hat with that on it," Skylar said.

KC still didn't laugh. Skylar and Daphne exchanged a look.

"KC?" Daphne said.

Finally KC looked them in the eye. "That couple with the stroller I went to talk to yesterday? Before we had lunch at the Boathouse?"

Daphne and Skylar nodded.

"That wasn't their baby. It was their *grandchild*. Their *third*. You should have seen their faces when I told them I was pregnant—at my age. It was a mix of disbelief and … pity. I've been trying not to think about it, but after that dream I can't seem to *stop* thinking about it."

"I know how that goes," Daphne said.

Skylar waved a dismissive hand. "They're probably from the Midwest. People have kids super early in the Midwest."

Daphne nodded. "True, but *you* can be like a California celebrity. California celebrities—actually celebrities everywhere it seems—are always having kids in their forties."

"Just please don't give yours a ridiculous name the way celebrities do, like Raisin or Zeus or something equally absurd," Skylar said. "Promise me that?"

This time Daphne laughed, but KC again ignored the joke. "That couple was from Kansas. They were here to meet their new granddaughter and then on their way to go traveling in Europe. Max and I are never going to be able to do anything like that now," she said.

"Do you and Max *want* to do something like that? I thought you were happy ensconced in your little bungalow on the beach," Daphne said.

"We are. But we've also talked about picking up one day and doing something a little out there, you know, like maybe renting an RV and visiting all the baseball stadiums in the United States."

Skylar made a horrified face. "I literally can't think of one thing I'd rather do less than that." Then she flicked a kitchen towel at Daphne. "And yes, I realize that makes me sound like a snob."

Daphne smiled, relieved that things between them were back to normal. "I guess I'm a snob too, because I wouldn't want to do that either."

"You guys know what I mean," KC said. "We love to go camping and hiking, for example. How are we going to go camping and hiking with a baby?"

"I'm pretty sure you can take a baby camping and hiking. It's not like there's a law against it or anything," Skylar said.

KC looked at them. "Do you think everyone's going to make fun of me for being an old mom? Do you think everyone's going to think the baby was an accident?"

"Screw them if they do," Skylar said. "No one blinks when an older *man* has a baby, but when a woman does it's sacrilegious? That's a stupid double standard, just like we were talking about the other night with Krissa. You think anyone's going to make fun of Max for becoming a dad again in his fifties? Hell no! If anything they'll be calling him a stud," Skylar said.

"Yeah, but—"

"Since when do you care about what other people think anyway?" Daphne said. "That's what we love about you, KC. You live your life in a way that makes *you* happy. That's the only playbook that matters to you. And given how happy you *usually* are, I'd say you're doing a pretty good job of executing that game plan. Why stop now? You're in incredible shape not just for *your* age, but for *any* age. Who says you can't have a baby in your forties?"

"Plus you could still pass for thirty." Skylar lightly *whapped* KC on the arm. "Don't forget that. And I hate you for it, by the way."

"Thanks. Max is in pretty good shape too. I always tell him he could pass for forty."

"James isn't in very good shape. He has a nice build and wears clothes well, but underneath he's soft and lazy, like me. God, I love him for that," Skylar said.

"So no five a.m. spinning classes for him then?" Daphne asked.

Skylar coughed and put a hand on her chest. "Oh God, no. Can you imagine? The only runs he goes on are to the donut store on Sunday mornings. Then it's back to bed with me and the newspaper."

"James is one lucky guy." Daphne said, then turned to KC. "And Max is a lucky guy too. You know what *I* think?"

"What?" KC asked.

"I think you need to go for a run. One, it will help you feel like yourself again, because *not* exercising is clearly dragging you down emotionally. And two, feeling like yourself again will show you that having a baby will only change who you are if you let it."

Skylar looked at Daphne. "That was profound."

"Thanks. It took me way too long to learn it for myself after I had Emma, but I finally did."

"I do miss running," KC said wistfully.

"Of course you do. You're half human, half tread-mill," Skylar said. She patted Daphne's arm. "I agree with Confucius here. I say get out there and do your thing!"

"You don't have to go balls-out or anything, but if your own doctor isn't telling you not to break a sweat, if I were in your shoes, I would be lacing them up," Daphne said. "And yes, that was an intentional use of the figurative and the literal for effect."

Skylar whistled and gave Daphne's arm a gentle push. "Profound *and* poetic. See? I *told* you you're a good writer."

"Maybe I should write a book about this weekend," Daphne said. "There's sure enough drama flying around."

"I love that idea! What would you call my character?" Skylar asked.

Daphne paused and pressed a finger against her chin. "I'm thinking Annie. She *is* the most famous redhead of all time."

Skylar laughed. "I'm okay with that if it will get you to keep writing."

"You really believe in me that much?"

Skylar narrowed her eyes. "You really want to have this conversation again?"

Daphne held up her hands. "I can see why you have so many people working for you. You're somehow terrifying yet motivating at the same time."

"If I worked for you, would you let me wear workout clothes to the office?" KC asked.

"I'm pretending I didn't hear that," Skylar said.

● ● ●

After they finished their coffee, KC stood up and gestured to Daphne. "You'd better get changed. You can't go running in your pajamas now, can you?"

Daphne raised her eyebrows. "Does this mean what I think it does?"

"Is your inner exercise addict about to bust out?" Skylar said.

KC grinned.

"Thank God for that, because you were kind of acting like a robot for a while there," Skylar said. "I say that with love, by the way."

"Love received." KC clapped her hands together, twice, Skylar style. "Now chop chop. Let's go. Time's a-wasting. Remember the flood!"

Daphne squinted at her. "Remember the what?"

"It's something my dad used to say when we were little. If he wanted us to hurry up and get out of the house or into the car or something, he would clap his hands and yell, 'Step to, people! Remember the flood!' I never had a clue what it meant, but it always got us moving," KC said.

"Well, apparently it worked, because you've never *stopped* moving," Daphne said. "Looks like we've unleashed the beast."

Skylar stood up and reached for her laptop. "Ain't that the truth? Prego's definitely got her mojo back. Don't go running a marathon or anything, ladies. We have another full schedule ahead of us, starting with brunch."

"We have to return all that stuff I bought too," Daphne said.

Skylar snapped her fingers. "We'll do that before we eat. Now, what are you two waiting for? Scoot!"

# Chapter Seventeen

"I'm getting French toast, three scrambled eggs with buttered toast, and a side of bacon," KC said before they even sat down at the restaurant. "And maybe a side of hash browns too."

"Hungry much?" Skylar asked as the hostess led them to their table.

"Yeah, what happened to 'I'm so full I'm never eating again'?" Daphne asked.

"That was last night! Today's a brand-new day and a brand-new appetite. Besides, I'm eating for two, remember?"

"Yeah, but your baby is what, the size of a garbanzo bean? How much can it possibly eat?" Skylar said.

"What can I say? We're starving."

"She's starving because she ran for a full thirty minutes *after* I thought our run was done," Daphne said. "Actually, what am I saying? *My* run *was* done."

"What do you mean?" Skylar asked.

"I mean when we got back to your building after running the three miles we'd agreed upon, KC announced that she wanted to keep going, so I popped into the coffee house next door and waited for her to come back. The lattes are really tasty there, by the way."

"I had some energy to burn. What can I say?" KC said.

"I take it you felt good on your return-to-exercise thing, then?" Skylar said.

KC grinned. "Like my old self again. Thanks for the push."

After they ordered, Daphne gestured toward the entrance. "Hey, there's Krissa. I wonder how her date went."

Skylar rubbed her hands together. "This should be good. A little entertainment with our meal."

KC poked Skylar's side. "You're assuming her date was no good? Isn't that a little pessimistic?"

"Pessimistic? No. Realistic? Yes. I'm just going with the odds, based on her track record."

"Dating in New York City sounds like navigating a minefield. Or playing Frogger," Daphne said.

"Hey lady! Have a seat and join the party. We just ordered. How was your date?" Skylar said as Krissa approached the table.

"Did it go well? The people want to know," KC said.

Krissa sat down and reached for a large glass of water, then proceeded to down it without stopping. As she did so, Skylar gave KC an *I told you so* nod. "See?"

"See what?" KC said.

Skylar motioned to the water glass Krissa was still chugging. "She's dehydrated. Dehydrated on a Sunday morning usually means late night plus alcohol consumption, and those two combined usually equals good date story. Am I right, Krissa? Is there a good story coming our way?"

Krissa finished the water and set the empty glass down. "Affirmative. Can I order first? I'm starving."

•   •   •

After they'd all been served, Krissa picked up her coffee mug and looked at the others. "Okay, ready to hear it?"

Daphne, KC, and Skylar all nodded, eyes expectant.

"Alrighty then, here goes. So I met this guy, Alan, for drinks. I think he was a real estate broker, or maybe a leasing agent? Something like that. I can't remember anymore. They're all beginning to blend together at this point. Anyhow, it was fun enough, not *amazing* or anything, but I was having a decent enough time—and had been drinking heavily, obviously—so I made an executive decision to sleep with him. Granted, it's not my style to have drunk sex with men on the first date, but I hadn't been with anyone since the cheater-who-will-remain-nameless, so I figured it was time to break the seal, so to speak."

"You made an *executive decision*. How official of you," Skylar said.

Krissa cut a piece of pancake with her fork. "I thought so too. I knew I had to get back on the horse at some point, so I figured I should do it with this real-estate guy given how slim the pickings have been recently. Getting over that *hump*, no pun intended, should make me less

139

freaked out when it comes time to do some humping for *real*, you know, with a guy I actually *like*."

Daphne started laughing. "So what happened after you made the *executive decision?*"

Krissa took a sip of her coffee. "We went back to his place and did it, and then …"

"And then *what?*" Skylar said.

Krissa set down her mug and glanced around. "And then … I kind of freaked out."

"Freaked out *how?*" Daphne asked.

Krissa nibbled on her thumbnail.

"Well?" Skylar made a *keep going* motion.

"I told him I was getting up to use the bathroom, discreetly grabbed my clothes, and left."

"You *left?* As in you left his *apartment?*" KC said.

Krissa nodded, a crooked smile on her face. "I totally bolted! As soon as it was over, I had this overwhelming urge to get the hell out of there. So I got the hell out of there, like a rat running for the highlands in a tsunami."

"I can't believe that's a true story," Daphne said, still laughing.

Krissa was laughing now too. "I know, right? I can't believe it either, but given that I did it, I guess I kind of have to. Mind you, I'm well aware that my behavior was completely psychotic and juvenile, but at the time I couldn't help myself."

Skylar pointed to Daphne. "See? Psychotic and juvenile happens sometimes. It's not the end of the world."

Daphne smiled and mouthed the words *I love you.*

*Right back at ya*, Skylar mouthed back.

"Are you going to reach out to him?" KC asked Krissa.

Krissa shook her head. "This morning he sent me a message through the dating site with a bunch of question marks. That was the entire message—a string of question marks."

"How did you reply?" Daphne asked.

Krissa made a guilty face. "I didn't. I blocked him."

"No way! That's so mean. Hilarious, but so mean," Skylar said.

"I know! I'm totally going to hell, but I just couldn't deal." Krissa looked at Daphne and KC. "I *swear* I'm normally a very nice person. And relatively sane."

"Well, even though you didn't demonstrate as much grace as you would have liked, at least the cheater's not the last guy you slept with anymore," Skylar said to Krissa. "Gotta look at the big picture, right?"

"That's the way I'm rationalizing it. I think of that status like the high score in a video game. I wanted to bump that lying cheater out of the top spot."

"Please tell us you have another date tonight," KC said. "I'm loving these stories."

Krissa moved her hands like a blackjack dealer leaving the table. "*Negative.* Tonight I'm nerding out with my cats and watching trash TV with a cheap bottle of wine and a tub of Dibs. But enough about me and my ridiculousness. How is the big weekend going?" Krissa asked the trio. "Any wild stories?"

Skylar shook her head. "Wild? No. Dramatic? A little. But it's all good now, right ladies?" She made slightly prolonged eye contact with both KC and Daphne, as if indicating that the connection between the three of them had grown even deeper.

Both nodded, their bond of friendship intact.

Daphne felt a rush of affection for Skylar as she fumbled in her purse for her phone, then scrolled through the photos. "Look at the wedding dress Skylar picked out! Isn't it stunning?" She handed the phone to Krissa.

"Wow, stunning is right. Well done," Krissa said.

"James is going to fall over when he sees her walking down the aisle. Tell him not to lock his knees, Skylar. Grooms pass out all the time because of that. It's a real thing," KC said.

Skylar laughed. "I'll try to remember to warn him."

Krissa handed the phone back, but before Daphne put it into her purse she looked through some of the other photos she'd recently taken. She came across one of her and Derek during his last trip to Columbus. They were at Jeni's, her favorite ice cream spot in town. She scrolled through a few other pictures from his visit before tucking the phone away, feeling a pang of guilt for still not having called him.

Krissa tapped Skylar on the arm. "Hey, speaking of James, I almost forgot to tell you. I saw the Ice Princess last night."

Skylar gave her a confused look. "You saw Sloane? Are you sure?"

"Pretty sure. Granted, I'd had a few drinks, but it wasn't like I was seeing double or anything."

"Where were you?"

"On the Upper West Side. Real-estate guy and I were crossing the street, I think at Broadway and Eighty-Fourth or right around there? It looked like she was coming out of the movie theater."

"Who was she with?"

"I didn't notice because of the crowd, sorry. But I'm ninety-nine percent sure it was Sloane."

Skylar furrowed her brow. "Why would she say she was going to the Catskills with her friends?"

"You think maybe she was on a date?" Daphne asked.

"Hmm. Maybe she's seeing someone she doesn't want you and James to know about," Krissa said.

"Possibly. She's not too forthcoming with details about her personal life," Skylar said.

"*Maybe* it's someone from the wrong side of the tracks," KC said, her eyes suddenly growing wide. "Like a convicted felon or something. Or maybe he's one of her friends' ex-boyfriends. *Or maybe* he's one of her professors at Columbia and is married with his own family in New Jersey!"

"Thank you. That's very helpful," Skylar said.

KC made a sheepish face. "Sorry, I kind of got a little carried away there."

Krissa waved a hand. "I'm sure it's nothing. She probably had a lot of studying to do so decided to stay in town. Columbia's packed to the gills with brainiacs. I'm sure there's a ton of pressure on those kids to keep up, even in summer school."

"Did you know Daphne almost went to Columbia?" Skylar asked KC.

"No. Really?" KC looked at Daphne.

Daphne nodded. "I didn't think I could handle living in such a big city back then. I think I made the right call, because I'm not even sure I could handle living in such a big city *now*."

"Stop it. I bet you'd thrive here," Skylar said.

"Maybe," Daphne said.

"I wouldn't thrive here. No way," KC said. "I need a beach within walking distance."

"Want to see the campus? We can go check it out this afternoon if you want," Skylar said. "It's really pretty."

"I'd love that," Daphne said.

Suddenly Skylar's eyes lit up. "Hey, I have an idea! Sloane lives right near there, so maybe I can drop off a goodie basket with her doorman. I can include a note saying that the treats are to help numb the pain of having to get back to studying after being away with her friends for the weekend. That way she won't know that *I know* she's still in town. What do you think? Do you think she'd like that?"

"A goodie basket? Who *wouldn't* like that? I think it's a great idea," Daphne said.

"I agree one hundred percent. One cannot go wrong by giving junk food to a college student," Krissa said.

"I sent care packages to Josh and Jared all the time when they were in school. They loved them," KC said.

"Cool. Let's do it. We can go up there before dinner," Skylar said. "We'll take the *subway*."

Krissa looked at her sideways. "Since when do you take the subway?"

"Since today. But *only* today." Skylar smirked at Daphne.

"Say what?" Krissa said.

Daphne laughed. "It's kind of a long story."

# Chapter Eighteen

"There are few things I enjoy in life more than getting pampered at a spa," Skylar said as they entered an empty sauna. "How were your treatments? Mine were heavenly."

KC stretched out on her back. "Soooooo relaxing. I could fall asleep right here."

"Please don't fall asleep in a sauna. I don't want you to, you know, *die*," Skylar said. "We've already been through that scare. What about you, Daphne?"

Daphne grimaced as she sat down. "My facial was great, but the massage … Good lord, that tiny little woman beat me up pretty bad. I had no idea hands that small could inflict so much damage."

KC laughed. "My massage lady was crazy strong too! Did she go super deep into your glutes? I thought it felt great."

"Is *glute* a fancy word for butt? Then yes, she went super deep, but it did *not* feel great. In fact, aside from giving birth, I think that was the most painful thing I've ever experienced," Daphne said.

Skylar rolled her eyes. "You need to toughen up, Whiney McGee. Massage is good for you."

"Easy for you to say—you didn't just get assaulted. You have no idea what that lady just did to my butt. I'm glad *I'm* not paying for that torture session," Daphne said.

"Ah, *now* you're happy I'm picking up the check." Skylar snapped a towel at her.

Daphne laughed and snapped a towel back. "You know it."

"I like it when your feisty side comes out. I should tick you off more often," Skylar said.

"Maybe you should," Daphne said.

KC sat up and frowned. "Is having a baby really *that* painful?"

Still laughing, Daphne shook her head. "Forget that I said that. It doesn't hurt *at all*." Then she looked at Skylar and mock whispered, "You can also call me *Fibby McFibberson* if you want."

"I heard that," KC said as she lay back down. "You could at least humor me, you know."

Skylar flicked her towel at KC. "You can take it, Wonder Woman."

Daphne adjusted her towel around her torso and leaned her back against the wall. "This is nice. Hanging out with you two again, chatting about everything and nothing, just like old times."

KC held up her wrist, her eyes still closed. "The clear beads."

"Say what?" Skylar said.

"The clear beads of the bracelet. They're here to remind us to savor moments like this. The *in-betweens*, remember?"

Daphne closed her eyes. *Savor the clear beads.*

The three of them settled into a comfortable silence for several moments—until Skylar suddenly broke it. "Can I confess something?"

"Of course," Daphne said, curious what Skylar could possibly have to confess.

Skylar scratched her cheek. "I'm not really sure how to say this, so I'm just going to blurt it out. Okay, here goes. I'm terrified that I'm going to sabotage things with James and lose him."

"What?" Daphne opened her eyes.

KC sat up. "Why would you sabotage things?"

"Because I think he's going to wake up one day and realize that he doesn't really love me. If *I* sabotage our relationship first, that won't happen."

"What are you talking about? Why would you think something like that?" Daphne asked.

Skylar stared at her hands. "Because … no man has ever loved me before. I mean *really* loved me."

"So what?" Daphne said. "You've never been in a serious relationship before."

Skylar shook her head. "You're not getting what I'm saying. I mean that … I think that … I think that, deep down, I'm afraid that no man *could* ever really love me. That maybe I've been on my own for so long because I'm … unlovable."

Daphne put a hand on Skylar's arm. "You don't really feel that way, do you?"

Skylar looked at her, and Daphne saw tears in her eyes.

"Oh, Skylar," she whispered.

"I know it sounds pathetic. I *know* that. But I can't help feeling that way. I know I've always said I don't *want* to be in a serious relationship, but the truth is that I'm *petrified* of being in one. I'm afraid that I'm not ... *capable* of being in one. That love is the one thing I've failed at, that I can't *win* at ... no matter how much I want to." She cleared her throat. "*There*. I said it. I'm a crazy person. My competitive nature has turned me into a crazy person."

Daphne was dumbstruck. The impression she'd always had of Skylar's love life was that Skylar was always in complete control, not afraid of rejection. Not even *remotely* afraid of rejection.

KC scooted closer to Skylar and put an arm around her. "It's not that you've failed at love, Skylar. It's that you haven't even let yourself *compete*. Think of how many guys you've turned away over the years."

"Maybe. But even so, I'm afraid that eventually James will get tired of my quirks and idiosyncrasies—but I'm too set in my ways to change them now. Plus, loath as I am to admit it, there's also the fear that eventually he'll want someone younger."

"I thought you've always kept men at arm's length because you weren't interested in *them*, not so you couldn't get hurt," Daphne said.

"I guess it's a combination of both," Skylar said.

"Have you *ever* been hurt?" Daphne asked.

Skylar shook her head. "I've never let anyone get close enough to hurt me. But I know James could, and I'm scared out of my mind that I'll fall apart if he leaves me."

"But he *loves* you, Skylar," Daphne said. "He's not going to leave you."

"I know he loves me today, but that's *today*. What if his feelings change tomorrow? What if he wakes up one day and decides he's sick of my morning breath or obsession with punctuality and then, *poof*, I'm alone again?"

"You can't think like that," KC said. "That's why they call love a leap of faith. There's no guarantee it's going to work out—not for anyone."

"I know, but I can't help it. It's like I'm doing everything I can to convince myself that we're doomed. I think that's why I wanted to make myself buy a wedding dress this weekend, like that would make it real—or something."

"What do you mean?" Daphne asked.

"You're going to think I'm a nut job if I tell you," Skylar said.

"No, we won't," Daphne said.

"Never," KC said.

Skylar sighed. "I told you guys we haven't set a date because we're too busy, but that's not the real reason … the real reason is because I keep dragging my feet. James said he'd be happy to get married whenever I want. He'd probably get married tomorrow if I asked him to."

"Then why are you so worried? That doesn't make any sense," KC said.

"I know it doesn't. I can't bring myself to set a date, because for some twisted reason I feel like if I *don't* set a date, then he can't call it off. Like I'll still be in control or something. I know, it's insane. I'm too scared to set a date for my own wedding."

"Why did you wait until now to tell us all this?" Daphne said.

Skylar gave her a wry smile, tears still in her eyes. "You're really asking me that? Because I was *embarrassed.* I think you know a little something about that?"

Daphne laughed weakly. "You're right. I'm an idiot. I'm sorry."

"Don't apologize. I know you're just trying to understand," Skylar said.

"I don't think you have anything to worry about with James," Daphne said. "Especially after seeing that picture in your closet."

"What picture?" KC asked.

"There's a framed photo of the two of them in Skylar's walk-in closet. He's smiling at her, and she's smiling back and laughing." She tapped Skylar's arm. "What did you say about him? That he makes you laugh so hard sometimes you can't breathe?"

Skylar nodded.

"Well, it sure looked like you were having trouble breathing in that photo," Daphne said.

Skylar chuckled. "We were at some super-boring fundraiser, and he kept whispering knock-knock jokes to keep me entertained. They were so stupid but *so* funny. I remember dabbing my eyes with a napkin to stop my mascara from running because I was laughing so hard. I guess somewhere in there the event photographer snapped a photo."

"I want to see it!" KC said.

"Do you realize how *rare* a connection like that is, Skylar? How *amazing* that is?" I was married for almost fifteen years and never once laughed hard enough to run my mascara. With you two, yes. With Brian, no," Daphne said.

"Really?" Skylar said.

"Nope. Not once. You and James obviously have something special."

"Okay, but ..." Skylar began.

Daphne held up a hand. "I'm not done. In addition to the picture that says a thousand words, not only did James ask you to *marry* him after just a few months of dating, he bought an *apartment* with you. That's a pretty major indication that he wants you around."

"I agree with Daphne. Sounds to me like he's in it for the long haul—and then some," KC said.

"You two are the best. Thanks. And I *know* how lucky I am, I do. The thing is, it's so good I'm afraid it's *too* good. I really love him, and even though rationally I understand what you're saying, I'm still terrified I'm going to do something to ruin it, to push him away first before he changes his mind about me."

"You need to trust in yourself more," Daphne said.

Skylar bit her thumbnail. "Can I confess something else?"

"Do you even have to ask?" KC said.

"Okay, this may sound silly, but with almost every guy I've dated, at some point I've tried to imagine him waiting for me at the end of the aisle. You know, at our wedding? But I've never been able to do it. It's like my brain wouldn't allow me to visualize it. Instead of a face, all I'd see was a big round blur perched on top of a tuxedo. But when I met James, almost right away I could picture him standing at the altar, like he was *meant* to be there."

"Then maybe he *is*," KC said.

"Skylar, I wish you could see this from our perspective. See how *positive* this all looks. Please try not to let your mind play tricks on you," Daphne said.

"I know I'm being ridiculous, but I can't help it. I think maybe that's why Sloane doesn't like me. She can smell my fear."

"You mean like a dog?" KC asked.

Skylar laughed. "I guess so, but she's way too pretty to be compared to a dog. I just wish I could explain to her that I'm not trying to replace her mother, that I'd just like to be her friend."

"She'd be lucky to have you as a friend," Daphne said. "I bet she'll see that eventually and warm up to you."

"Hey, speaking of friends, can I say something about why the three of us are together this weekend?" KC asked Skylar.

"Of course," Skylar said.

"All right, here goes. Maybe I'm being nitpicky, but you've been pretty adamant that it's perfectly fine to have a kid in your forties, right? That I'm healthy and happy and it's *my* life so I should ignore what anyone else thinks or says about it, right?"

"Right," Skylar said.

"So then why the aversion to calling this a bachelorette weekend? What's so wrong with that? Who *cares* if you're in your forties, Skylar? You're engaged to be *married*, and that's worth celebrating with a proper name. So can we agree that Daphne and I are in this wonderful city called New York for the *bachelorette party* of our dear friend Skylar, whom we love and adore?"

Skylar held up her hands. "Okay, okay, fine. You've made your case. We'll call it a bachelorette weekend or bachelorette party, or whatever you want. Now let's get out of here before we sweat to death."

# Chapter Nineteen

"What do college students like to eat?" Skylar scanned the options as they patrolled the aisles of a Whole Foods on the Upper West Side. "Are cookies and brownies and microwave popcorn still good?"

"Those are always good. And *oooh*, get Swedish Fish too!" KC said. "That would be a nice touch since we mentioned those to her yesterday."

"Sloane's pretty thin. You think she even *eats* junk food?" Daphne asked.

"Everyone eats junk food," KC said.

Daphne looked at KC. "Do you?"

KC nodded. "Not very often, but once in a while, for sure. The key to good health is not to deprive yourself of anything. That's my motto—especially now that I'm pregnant."

"You *have* been eating a lot of crappy food this weekend," Skylar said.

"My personal vice is Doritos," Daphne said.

"I love Doritos!" KC said. "Nacho Cheese or Cool Ranch?"

"Is that even a question? Nacho Cheese, obviously," Daphne said.

"Do they sell Doritos and Swedish Fish at Whole Foods? And am I getting too much stuff here?" Skylar tossed a handful of individually wrapped brownies into the basket, which was now nearly full.

"Highly doubtful that they sell anything resembling Doritos or Swedish Fish at a store like this, but I saw a CVS down the street," Daphne said. "As for having too much stuff, she can always share the treats with her friends, just like you were talking about yesterday. It will be like a reincarnation of our marathon cram sessions."

Skylar reached for a bag of chocolate-covered pretzels. "You're right! Let's fill this baby up to the rim, then top if off with some Swedish Fish and Doritos—Nacho Cheese *and* Cool Ranch. Maybe showering her and all her friends with study snacks will force her to like me, kind of a food bribe, if you will."

"I'm getting hungry," KC said.

•  •  •

"What a pretty campus." KC craned her neck to take in the main quad, then pointed to the columns and rotunda-style crown of the Low Memorial Library. "Some of the buildings remind me of the ones in Washington, DC. Doesn't that one look like the Jefferson Memorial?"

Daphne turned her head as if on a swivel, amazed by how insulated, how *protected* the Columbia campus felt from the outside world. "It's gorgeous. I can't believe we're still in New York City. It's like a sanctuary here." Despite the fact that it was summer—and a Sunday at that—the campus was still buzzing with activity, a steady stream of backpack-wearing students milling along the walkways, others lazily splayed out on the grass to enjoy the afternoon sunshine.

Skylar pointed toward the western gate, then to Broadway just beyond it. "Hard to believe right out there is one of the busiest streets in the world, right?" She looked at Daphne. "*Still* think you wouldn't have been able to handle going to school here?"

"I'm not sure. Manhattan may have been too daunting for me, especially at that age—but maybe if I'd stayed inside the fortress walls I'd have been okay." Daphne imagined herself as a teenager, sitting quietly on the grass with a notebook jotting down ideas for a story—perhaps about how a single decision could dramatically affect a young woman's life. "It does seem like we're in our own little world right now."

"I guess in a way every college is its own little world—or maybe that's just youth itself. Come on, let's walk around for a little while before we head over to Sloane's," Skylar said.

# Chapter Twenty

"Nice digs for a college student," KC said as they entered the lobby of Sloane's building, a modern high-rise a few blocks west of campus.

"It's easy to live well when your dad's paying the bills," Skylar said with a shrug.

"Does she have roommates?" Daphne asked.

"She did in the dorms for a year, but since then she's lived here alone, in a one bedroom. I've never been invited up to see it, though."

"Maybe her secret ex-con married professor boy-friend lives with her," KC said with an evil grin.

"Will you stop with the conspiracy theories already? I'm paranoid enough here," Skylar said.

"Sorry. I'm not sure what's gotten into me. It must be the pregnancy hormones."

Skylar approached the doorman's station to drop off the care package, and then returned a moment later with a relieved—and hopeful—look on her face. "Okay, it's done! Maybe that will help thaw things a little bit." She glanced at her watch. "Should we head down to the Theater District? We've got some time to kill, so we can do a little window-shopping before the show."

"Window-shopping, yes. Regular shopping, definitely not!" Daphne said. "If I even *look* like I'm about to reach for my credit card, one of you needs to physically restrain me, okay?"

"I'll do it. I'm stronger than I look," KC said.

The three of them headed for the lobby door, but before they reached it a young woman walked in, carrying a plastic bag from Popeyes Chicken.

It was Sloane.

"Well, hello there!" Skylar said a bit louder than was necessary, again clearly nervous.

Sloane froze, her fair cheeks taking on a pink hue. "What are you doing here?" She tucked the bag behind her back, but they'd all seen it.

Skylar gestured toward the doorman's station. "I left you a little something to help you with your studying, since you mentioned you had that exam coming up."

Sloane's eyes followed Skylar's and locked in on the basket, which Skylar had decorated with a large yellow bow. "Oh, that was nice of you."

"It's my pleasure. I know I went a little overboard, but Daphne and KC reminded me that you could always share the treats with your friends—just like we used to do during our own study sessions."

"Of course. Thank you," Sloane said.

An awkward pause followed as the four of them stood there by the door. Daphne wondered if Sloane was going to explain why she wasn't in the Catskills. She thought maybe she was waiting for Skylar to ask her about it.

Before the silence went on too long, Skylar spoke again. "My friend Krissa thought she saw you at a movie theater last night, so I thought I'd drop off the basket for you today in case she was right. You know, if for whatever reason you'd stayed in town. Daphne and KC wanted to see the Columbia campus anyway, so since we were coming all the way up here, it was no trouble."

*There, she'd brought it up.*

Daphne looked at Sloane, the ball now in her court.

Sloane swallowed, her cheeks still flushed. "Yeah … um, I decided to stick around after all. Lots of studying to do, you know."

Daphne and KC exchanged a quick glance. Daphne was no expert in body language, but it was pretty obvious to her that Sloane wasn't telling the truth. She waited for Skylar to respond, wondering if she'd push the issue or let it slide.

Skylar hesitated briefly before dropping it. "Okay. Well, we'll let you get to it, then. I know you have a lot to do."

"Good luck on your exam," Daphne said.

"Enjoy the snacks," KC said with a wave.

"Thanks." Sloane headed toward the doorman's station.

They were on their way outside when Skylar suddenly turned around. "Sloane?"

Sloane turned around too, holding the basket. "Yes?"

Skylar cleared her throat. "I … I just want you to know that if there's ever anything you'd like to tell me, I'm all ears." The tone of her voice was friendly, non-accusatory, gentle even. Daphne was impressed that

Skylar had knocked on that door and was curious to see Sloane's response. Would she open it? Daphne herself doubted that Sloane would be forthcoming about her mystery boyfriend—or maybe girlfriend?—if she indeed had one. But she admired the effort Skylar was making to connect with her future stepdaughter.

Sloane let out an audible sigh, which startled Daphne. "Will you please just let it go? Please?"

Skylar was also thrown by the remark. "Let what go?"

"I'm not an idiot, okay? I know what you're doing. What you're trying to get me to admit. Will you please give it a rest?"

Now Skylar was the one whose cheeks began to flush. "I'm sorry for meddling. I just thought … I just wanted you to know that if, um, you're seeing someone, there's no need to keep it a secret."

A look of confusion flickered in Sloane's eyes, and she scoffed. "You think I'm *seeing* someone? You think *that's* why I didn't go to the Catskills?"

"No. Well … maybe. I mean, I've certainly canceled plans with friends to spend time with a boy before." She looked at Daphne and KC. "Remember how I ditched you guys homecoming weekend to go camping with Craig what's-his-name?"

Daphne and KC both nodded but didn't say anything, not wanting to intrude on the conversation.

Skylar turned back to Sloane. "I know I'm not doing a very good job of it, but what I'm saying, or *trying* to say, is that I'm here if you'd ever like to talk—about anything. And of course you're more than welcome to bring a friend to the apartment, whoever that person is."

Sloane slowly shook her head. "You really don't get it, do you?"

"Don't get *what*? I'm just trying to let you know that I remember what it's like to be in college, that's all."

"I'm well aware of that. You practically shove it in my face every time I see you," Sloane said.

"Oh. I didn't realize—"

Sloane sighed again. "You want me to just *say* it?"

Skylar nodded. Daphne nodded too, more confused than ever as to what was going on.

Sloane closed her eyes, and when she opened them they were filled with tears. "I don't have a *boyfriend*, Skylar. And I don't have a girlfriend either, if you were wondering about that too. I don't have *any* friends."

"What? What do you mean?" Skylar said.

"I *mean*, I didn't bail on my plans to go to the Catskills because I was never *invited* to go to the Catskills. I *mean*, I never invite anyone to the apartment to meet you and Dad because I don't *have* anyone to invite. *No one.* Is that clear enough? If it's not, your friend saw me at the movies last night because I was there *by myself*. I spent Saturday night of a three-day weekend, and will actually spend the *entire* weekend *by myself* because everyone took off in groups of friends—none of which included me because *I have no friends.*"

Skylar was speechless. For several seconds she just stood there like a deer in the headlights. Daphne and KC also remained silent.

"I had no idea," Skylar finally said in a near-whisper.

"Well, now you do. I made up the Catskills story so you and Dad wouldn't feel sorry for me, okay?"

Sloane then looked at Daphne and KC. "I'm sorry for being rude. It's been kind of a rough few days, and I wasn't expecting to see anyone right now, obviously." She held up the Popeyes Chicken bag for a moment, then let her arm hang by her side, looking tired—and defeated.

"Please don't worry about that," Daphne said. She imagined Emma in a similar situation and felt a stabbing sensation in her heart.

*How crushing to be so alone during what is supposed to be the best time of your life! How much must that hurt?*

Her four years in college hadn't been without drama or heartache, but the one constant had been the support of her friends. Seeing Sloane standing there in her flower-print slip dress, young and beautiful but with nowhere to go and a takeout order for one in her hand stirred Daphne's maternal instincts and made her want to protect the poor girl. She was tempted to take a step forward and hug her but refrained, knowing that if anyone was going to make that move, it needed to be Skylar.

"Has it always been like this for you?" Skylar asked.

Sloane shrugged. "At Columbia? Pretty much."

"Is it that hard to make friends there? Your dad said you had lots of friends in high school."

"That was high school."

"Oh," Skylar said.

Daphne waited for Skylar to ask the next question, the one they were all thinking, the one that needed to be asked.

"What changed?" Skylar asked.

Sloane stared at the floor for a moment, then nodded toward the elevators. "Do you want to come upstairs?"

•   •   •

Sloane unlocked her apartment door and gestured to the sofa and oversize chair in the tidy living room. "Can I offer you something to drink? Water? Soda?"

"I'd love some water, thanks," Skylar said. Daphne and KC both nodded in agreement, all three of them eagerly waiting to hear what Sloane had to say.

A few moments later, Sloane joined them in the living room with a tray and set it on the coffee table, then sat herself down with a thud. "You really want to know why I don't have any friends? It's not a pretty story."

Skylar's voice softened. "Of course I do, honey."

Daphne was startled by the term of endearment. She'd heard Skylar call her and KC *honey* countless times, but to hear her use it to address Sloane showed a side of Skylar that Daphne hadn't seen. It sounded … maternal. Daphne felt her lips curl up into a tiny smile and turned her head so no one would think she was making light of the situation.

*She's going to be a good stepmom*, she thought.

Sloane began to speak, her words halting. "Okay, here goes … I went to a tiny private high school with all girls, so I never really learned how to socialize with boys. I didn't drink, and I had never even been on a real date. But when I got to college everything was different, and everyone was so much more experienced than I was. So I wanted to, you know, fit in." She paused and took a sip of water before continuing. "Early on in my freshman year, I tagged along to a frat party with some girls from my dorm. They were kind of the popular crew, you know? Fun and pretty and outgoing and all that, so I was hoping they would invite me to join their group. Anyhow, when we got to the party I was nervous. I had a drink and it made me feel better, so I had a couple more. More than a couple more, actually … and somehow I ended up making out with this guy, his name was Chad, in front of everyone."

"We've all done that," Skylar said.

"But what I didn't know was that one of the girls from my dorm, Liza, had a huge crush on Chad. She had come to the party specifically to run into him. I guess they'd hooked up a couple times. She thought I knew, so she was livid. *Livid.* But I didn't know. I swear I didn't know."

"Oh hon, of course you didn't," Skylar said.

"After that, Liza started spreading rumors on social media about how I liked to steal other people's boyfriends, that I'd slept with a bunch of guys on campus, blah blah blah. And everyone believed her. So before I knew it, the rumors were all over school and wouldn't go away. It was like it didn't matter that they weren't true." Sloane buried her face in her hands and quietly began crying.

Skylar looked at KC and Daphne, clearly unsure what to do.

Daphne mouthed the words *It's okay, let her talk.*

Sloane sniffled and wiped the tears away with the back of her hand. "I was quite the talk of campus for a while there. Even girls I'd been kind of friendly with would give me dirty looks and walk right by me as if we'd never met. So eventually I just stopped trying to talk to anyone."

"Oh, Sloane, I'm so sorry." Skylar whispered.

"People can be so cruel," Daphne said. She again imagined Emma in that situation and felt a rush of anger and disgust, of helplessness and angst all mixed together.

*Poor Sloane.*

KC frowned. "People can suck."

"Yes, they really can," Sloane said with a weak laugh. "And you know something else?"

They all looked at her.

"The nasty things people were saying about me? That I was a whore and a slut and a tramp? Until that night, I'd never even kissed a boy. And *he* never spoke to me after that."

Skylar tucked a lose strand of hair behind Sloane's ear. "I'm so sorry. I take it *this* is why you want to graduate early?"

Sloane nodded.

"Horrified as I am by what you've been through, I really admire you for holding yourself together and sticking with it," Skylar said.

"I'd probably have dropped out, myself," Daphne said.

"Does your dad know about this?" Skylar asked.

Sloane shook her head. "Would *you* want to tell your dad something like this?

Besides, it's not like he can do anything about it."

"I know it happened a while ago, but you could have talked to me," Skylar said.

Sloane coughed out a laugh. "Are you serious? Since the day I met you, you've gone on and on about how much you *loved* college, about the lifelong friendships you formed there, about *The Three Musketeers* and how everything back then was so wonderful and fun. What was I supposed to say?"

"I'm not sure. The truth, maybe?"

"I was too embarrassed to tell you the truth. Put yourself in my shoes, Skylar. You're a brilliant, beautiful, successful career woman with a fabulous life, and I'm a social pariah. I was afraid you'd see right through me if I even tried talking to you about *anything*, so it was easier to say nothing."

"Women. Why do we do this to ourselves?" Skylar said.

"Do what?" Sloane asked.

"Knock ourselves down, focus on our shortcomings instead of celebrating our accomplishments, secretly compare ourselves to our friends, pretend things are okay when they're not, think we're not deserving of love. Should I go on?"

Sloane blinked. "You do those things too?"

"To some degree we all do, at least sometimes," Skylar said.

"I thought you had it so together," Sloane said.

Skylar put an arm around Sloane's slender shoulders, then nodded toward Daphne and KC. "Do you know why I met these two amazing women when I did?"

"I thought you met in the dorms."

"Yes, but not right away. Shortly before my freshman year was about to start I got really sick with mono, so I had to enroll a quarter late. By that time everyone—including my roommate—had already formed cliques. So for weeks I literally had no friends. Zero. I thought I was going to love college, but instead it began as the loneliest time of my life."

"Really?" Sloane said.

"Really. I was *miserable.* Anyhow, after weeks of waiting for friends to magically appear I finally decided to go find some on my own. So one day I knocked on Daphne and KC's door and essentially asked if I could hang out with them. I'd never met either of them but had seen them together in the dining hall and thought they seemed friendly, like the kind of girls I would get along with."

"That's how you met?" Sloane said.

"She knocked right on our door and asked to be friends with us," KC said.

"I'd never felt so popular," Daphne said.

Skylar looked at Sloane. "What I'm trying to say is that, despite the appalling way you've been treated, one way or another you *will* find women who love and support you. It just may not happen the way you expected it to. And to be honest, if I hadn't met these two the way I did, I might not have appreciated their friendship as much as I do—and always will. Try as they might, they're never getting rid of me. Now, I know my experience in no way compares to yours, not even close, but please believe that things will eventually get better."

"I hope they will," Sloane said.

"They will, trust me. By the way, to clear up any remaining misconceptions that my college experience was without bumps in the road, let me tell you something else about it. This prestigious university you attend? The one at which you're getting amazing grades despite the emotional trauma you've been through? I didn't get in here."

"You didn't?" Sloane said.

"No. It was my first choice too. I was crushed."

"I never knew that!" Daphne said.

Skylar looked at Daphne. "I was didn't tell you because I knew *you* got in. I'm competitive, remember?"

Daphne was too surprised to respond.

Skylar turned back to Sloane. "Not that I didn't love my time at Northwestern—obviously after the rough start—I had the time of my life there. But before that I'd had my heart set on living in New York City, literally since I was like twelve years old, so it took a while to get used to the fact that I was going to have to wait a few years for that to happen."

"Well, you're here now, right?" KC said.

"Right. It worked out just swimmingly, in my opinion. Maybe not the way I'd envisioned at the outset, but in retrospect I wouldn't change a thing, because I love the way my life has turned out. In a way I love it *more* because the sorrow and disappointment I felt back then makes me treasure what I have now. That includes your dad, by the way. Meeting him at this age makes me appreciate him more than if I'd met him as a young pup. Believe me, I kissed a lot of toads before I stumbled upon him."

Sloane smiled. "He is a pretty good guy."

KC pointed toward the goodie basket on the coffee table. "Hey, speaking of swimming, can I have some of your Swedish Fish? I'm eating for two, and I'm starving."

Sloane laughed and held out an arm. "Have at it."

# Chapter Twenty-One

A half hour later the four of them were still in the living room of Sloane's apartment, the goodie basket on the mosaic tile coffee table markedly smaller, thanks in large part to KC's seemingly insatiable appetite.

"I can't believe *you* would be intimidated by *me,*" Sloane said to Skylar as she unwrapped a chocolate-chip cookie. "Don't you have like a really important job with a ton of people working for you?"

Skylar tipped her water glass toward Daphne and KC. "Ladies?"

"Totally intimidated. And she *never* gets intimidated, at least not that I've seen," Daphne said. "When we ran into you outside of her building, for us it was like watching a movie star be starstruck by another movie star."

KC popped a chocolate-covered pretzel into her mouth. "I'd never seen her so freaked out. It kind of freaked *me* out."

"I'm sorry I was rude to you," Sloane said, casting her eyes downward. "I guess it's become my defense mechanism, as my psychology professor would say."

"Don't apologize. I'm just glad the ice is officially broken," Skylar said.

Sloane looked up and gave her a shy smile. "I am too."

"Your apartment is adorable, Sloane. I love this furniture." Daphne ran a hand over the blue-and-white-striped oversize chair she was sitting on, and then nodded at the plush gray couch, which was adorned with pillows and knitted throw blankets of various colors and patterns. She stood up to admire a row of old-fashioned sconces flanking an oversize clock mounted on the wall behind the couch, then wandered across the hardwood floors to the opposite side of the room, where a number of framed black-and-white sketches of various New York neighborhoods were hung in a staggered formation. "Did you decorate it yourself? I'd never think to mix and match colors and styles like this."

Sloane nodded. "In my free time, which unfortunately I have a lot of, I go to antique shows, arts and crafts markets like the Brooklyn Flea, estate sales, things like that. I think it's fun to blend a contemporary style with a touch of, I don't know, vintage I guess?" She glanced around the room. "I'm not really sure what you'd call this look I have here. I was basically trying to warm up what was a blah space."

"Cozy chic?" KC touched a dark green, wooden magazine rack next to the couch. "Is cozy chic a look?"

"Whatever the name, it *looks* like it's out of a magazine," Daphne said. "The colors, the textures, the contrast of old and new—everything fits together so well."

"I wish I had that kind of creative vision," Skylar said. "My brain doesn't work that way at all. I'm a numbers person. Give me an Excel spreadsheet over a vision board any day of the week."

"I'm not a numbers person, but I'm not much of a decorator either," Daphne said with a frown.

Skylar pointed at her. "But you can piece ideas into stories. That's a different kind of decorating."

"I do like to weave a good story together," Daphne said.

"I have no eye for design whatsoever," KC said. "I guess that means I'm design blind?" She giggled at her own joke. "When Max and I moved into our place we drove to Ikea, pointed to a bunch of displays and said, 'We'll take that.' Then we drove straight home and set up everything exactly like it was in the store—before we forgot."

Daphne gave Skylar's foot a gentle kick. "I imagine you don't have anything from Ikea at your mansion."

"Not currently. But you never know. There's still some space to fill."

Daphne laughed. "That's an understatement."

KC glanced at the clock on the wall. "Is that time correct? What time does the show start?"

Skylar turned her head. "Oh no. Soon!" She reached for her purse and stood up. "Excuse me for a minute, will you?" She dug out her phone and held it to her ear as she walked toward the kitchen.

Daphne pretended to maneuver a steering wheel. "Calling a car I bet. Looks like we're done with taking the subway."

"I do like those fancy town cars she gets. I'm not gonna lie," KC said.

"What show are you seeing?" Sloane asked.

"*Hamilton*," Daphne said.

"Really? You'll love it." Sloane said.

"You've seen it?" KC said.

"My dad and Skylar took me for my birthday."

"Lucky girl," Daphne said.

"I know." Sloane frowned as a memory occurred to her. "Skylar said I could bring a friend, but I told her I didn't want to. Kind of abruptly, I think."

Daphne felt another maternal tug, knowing Sloane now realized how much she'd hurt Skylar's feelings over the past few months. She reached over and put a hand on Sloane's shoulder. "Don't worry about it. She understands."

"You think so?" Sloane said, a worried look in her eyes.

"I know so. Trust me, everything's going to be okay."

KC nodded. "Daphne's a mom. She knows these things."

"Thank you both," Sloane said. "You're very kind, I can see why Skylar cares about you so much."

Skylar emerged from the kitchen, her phone pressed to her ear. "Hey hot stuff. Are you sitting on your couch watching bad TV?"

Daphne and KC exchanged a look of confusion. Skylar clearly wasn't talking to a car service.

"Cool. Want to go see *Hamilton*?" Skylar said.

Pause.

"In forty-five minutes."

Daphne glanced at Sloane, who held up her hands as if to say *Don't ask me.*

"Great. Meet the ladies outside the theater. Tickets are at will call under my name. I'll give them your number, to be safe."

KC tapped Daphne's shoulder and whispered, "What's going on?"

"I'm as perplexed as you are," Daphne said.

"You're welcome, babe. Have fun, and I'll see you afterward." Skylar casually tossed her phone back into her purse, and then resumed her seat on the couch.

"What just happened?" Daphne asked.

Skylar reached for her water glass. "Oh, that? That was Krissa. She's going to *Hamilton* with you two."

"You're not coming?" KC said.

Skylar shook her head. "I'll meet you afterward. Right now I'm going to stick around and ask my talented future stepdaughter for some tips on how to make our apartment look a little less sterile." She turned to Sloane and raised an eyebrow. "*If* you're interested, of course. What do you say? Want to go buy some design magazines and grab a bite to eat and see if we can figure it out together? You can save that Popeyes Chicken for lunch tomorrow."

Sloane put a hand on her heart. "You want *my* advice on how to decorate your apartment?"

"Decorate, accentuate, pretty-up, whatever you'd like to call making it look much less barren than it currently does. *Yes.* Actually, now that I think about it, I'd love to tag along with you to one of those estate sales or flea markets and watch you work your magic. Maybe you could be my design consultant? Teach me a thing or two?"

"You really think I'm that talented?"

Skylar turned to Daphne and KC. "Do I mess around when it comes to things like this?"

"Skylar doesn't mess around when it comes to *anything*," Daphne said.

"I … I … don't know what to say," Sloane said.

"Say yes," Skylar said. "Or *sí*, or *oui*, or *ja*. Anything that indicates an affirmative response."

Sloane smiled. "I'd love to."

# Chapter Twenty-Two

"Oh my God, this food tastes so good!" KC said as she took another gargantuan bite of her hamburger.

She, Daphne, and Krissa were plowing through burgers and fries at the outdoor Shake Shack in Madison Square Park in the Flatiron District. They'd come straight from the show, and despite the hour, the area was still bustling with tourists and locals alike.

"Isn't it? And you know what else? I've heard from *two* fellow carnivores that the veggie burger here is worth giving up meat for, but the regular burgers are so incredible that I'm like, *why would I want to do that?*" Krissa said.

"Maybe you can get one of your dates to order the veggie burger, just so you can take a bite," Daphne said.

Krissa pointed a fry at her. "I like the way you think."

"Hey, there's Skylar!" KC waved in Skylar's direction as she approached from across the park.

"My personal interest notwithstanding, that was very cool of her to give up her ticket and stay with Sloane tonight," Krissa said as she reached for another fry. "I can't believe the Ice Princess isn't an ice princess after all."

"Not at all," Daphne said. "She seems like a sweet kid. Just got put through the ringer, unfortunately."

"Sounds like she was really being bullied, eh?" Krissa said.

"Bullies are the worst," KC said.

"I'd have fallen to pieces if that had happened to me in college," Daphne said. "I'd probably fall to pieces if it happened to me *now*. Just the thought of Emma in that situation makes me ill."

KC dipped a fry into ketchup. "I'm so glad social media didn't exist when we were that age. Seems like it's such a source of angst for younger people." She laughed. "Did I just say *younger people*? Maybe I *am* old enough to be a grandmother."

"Coolest grandma in town," Daphne said.

"With or without technology, some kids will always find a way to be cruel," Krissa said. "In law school, a friend told me that when she was sixteen some boys on the high school football team spread a rumor that she was sleeping with their math teacher because they thought his class was too hard and wanted him to get fired. She says it was a huge lie—but it worked! The poor teacher ended up resigning to avoid the stigma of the manufactured scandal."

KC's eyes got big. "Something like that happened at my high school too! Although in that case the teacher *was* sleeping with his student. I think she was a sopho-more, or maybe a junior? Regardless, she was definitely underage, and it was a huge scandal. He ended up in jail. Although now that I think about it, I guess that wasn't bullying, so I'm not sure why I even told that story. Sorry! I think I'm just so in love with this food I can't think straight."

Daphne laughed. "If Max were here I think he might be a little jealous of that hamburger."

Skylar appeared at their table. "Hi, ladies! How was the show?"

Daphne tapped her palms on the table and began to rap. "My name is Al-ex-and-er Ham-il-ton … I said my name is Al-ex-and-er Ham-il-ton."

Skylar sat down and reached for a fry. "Catchy tunes, eh? So you liked it?"

"Loved it!" KC said.

"I wish there had been a show like that when I was in school," Daphne said. "I'd probably remember a lot more of the history I was taught. Actually, I bet a lot of kids are going to *major* in history because of it."

"Like CSI! Remember when that show was in its heyday and everyone decided to major in forensic science?" KC said.

"I'm glad you enjoyed it," Skylar said to Daphne and KC, then turned to Krissa. "What about you? Did it live up to the hype?"

"It was genius. Much better than watching a *Naked and Afraid* marathon while swiping and scrolling through dating profiles and mowing through a carton of Dibs, which is what I was doing when you called—and would probably still be doing at this exact moment. Actually, that's not quite true. The Dibs would be long gone by now, and I'd probably have moved on to watching *Bar Rescue*, equally bad yet also addicting."

"I've never seen either of those shows," Daphne said.

"And you're better off for it," Krissa said.

"How'd things go with Sloane?" KC asked Skylar.

"Yes, do tell," Krissa said. "Your buddies here filled me in on the movie-of-the-week drama. I did *not* see that one coming."

"Really good, actually. After Daphne and KC left it was kind of awkward for a bit because we'd never spent any time alone together, but as we got to talking more, I realized how similar she and I are."

"You mean smart, driven, beautiful, and intimidating? I can see that," Daphne said.

"Skylar has a protégé. How cute. Your very own Mini-Me," Krissa said.

Skylar laughed. "I wouldn't go that far. She's like an inch taller than I am. And about fifteen pounds lighter, damn her."

"So she's going to help you decorate your apartment?" Daphne asked.

"Yep. God knows we need more stuff to fill it up, not to mention give it some charm to make it feel like a proper home. I think it will be fun for her, and a good way for us to spend some more time together—that's my sneaky plan. I know her dad will love having her around more too. Plus in my opinion she's got real talent, so I'm not asking for her help just to make nice. I'm legitimately impressed with what she's done with her place, and not for much money either. She has a real knack for finding interesting pieces that add a lot of flavor to a room and bringing it all together."

"Sounds like it could be a future career," KC said.

"How much longer does she have at school?" Daphne asked.

"Because she's taking summer school, just another year after this session ends. But I told her I think she should transfer, add some design classes to her schedule, and spend a full two years somewhere else. What's the point of being miserable where she is, right? If she wants to stay at a top school in New York she can go to NYU, but with her grades she can pretty much go anywhere she wants."

"I'm surprised she hasn't transferred already." Krissa yanked a thumb over her shoulder. "I would have gotten the hell out of there long ago if I'd been slut-shamed like that."

"Me too, but I think she's so beaten down emotionally that she doesn't believe she'd be capable of making friends anywhere, so she figures it's easier to just withdraw socially and wait it out. I wish she'd told her dad when it happened so he could have helped her push for some kind of justice, to do *something* to stand up to such abhorrent behavior. Not just to the girl who started the rumors, but the kids who helped spread them. I can't do anything about that now, but I *am* going to do my best to convince her that there's still time for her to enjoy what's left of her college experience. Who knows? She might even find her very own KC and Daphne."

"Aw, wouldn't that be cute? The Three Musketeers reincarnated." Krissa pretended to wipe a tear from her eye. "I wish I'd been part of your little gal crew in college. Maybe I'd be less neurotic."

"You were in elementary school when we were in college," Skylar said.

Krissa pointed a fry at her. "I was tall for my age. I could have tried to pass."

Skylar snatched the fry and popped it into her mouth. "Anyhow, I just think it would be such a shame for Sloane to leave this part of her life behind with such a bitter taste in her mouth when I *know* there are wonderful people out there she could be meeting and having fun with—friends who will make her feel good about herself, during the fun times and the not-so-fun times." She held up her wrist, pointed to her bracelet, and looked at KC. "I don't want her to miss out on the day-to-day experiences that make college so special. That make *life* so special."

KC grinned. "The clear beads."

Skylar winked at her. "The clear beads."

"Say what?" Krissa said.

Skylar ran her fingers over her bracelet and gave Krissa a quick explanation of the significance of its parts. When she was done she twisted her wrist back and forth. "Everyone deserves friends who help them appreciate what really matters—especially my future stepdaughter, right?"

Daphne nudged Skylar with her elbow. "Look at you, acting all maternal."

"I know. Who would have thought, right? I kind of like this side of myself."

"Even though that was pretty awkward when things came to a head earlier, I'm really glad you and Sloane finally cleared the air," KC said. "If she's anything like Max's sons were with me, it might take a while for her to feel *completely* comfortable around you, but she's going to be so happy to have you in her life. You just watch."

"Thanks pumpkin," Skylar said. She looked at Krissa. "I've had enough drama for one day, so let's lighten things up. How about it? Got any stories you haven't told me yet?"

"Oh yes, please tell us a story," KC said.

"You bet I do." Krissa reached for her phone. "You ready?"

KC rubbed her hands together. "You don't have to ask me twice."

"I feel like you're the gift that keeps on giving," Daphne said.

Krissa began tapping at her phone. "These aren't dating stories per se, rather messages I got today from a dating site." She held up the phone, and the three of them leaned in to see the screen. The man's username was NewYorkDevil, and his photo was of a half-naked man lying seductively on a bed ... next to a cat. His message said: *Are you ready to fall in love with me?*

Krissa pointed an angry finger at the screen. "*No,* naked cat guy! I am *not* ready to fall in love with you. I am *never* going to be ready to fall in love with you!"

"That's so creepy," Daphne said.

"Isn't it? Check out this one." Krissa tapped at her phone again, then held it up.

The message was from a heavyset, mustached man with the user name LoveFlame162. *Damn your sexy.*

Daphne frowned. "I hate when people mix up *your* and *you're.*"

"The worst, right?" Krissa rolled her eyes. "Lame screen name plus bad grammar plus cheesy message equals *the worst!*"

"And check out where he lives," KC pointed at the phone. "New Hampshire. I know I've never been that great at geography, but I'm pretty sure New Hampshire is more than a hop, skip, and a jump from New York City."

Skylar squinted. "Does that say *two hundred and sixty* miles away?"

"Yes!" Krissa made a *What the hell?* gesture with her free hand. "And it happens *all the time.* How are you supposed to meet someone who lives four hours away for a drink?"

"Is he divorced? I bet he's a divorced guy if he's living in the suburbs," Skylar said.

"They're *all* divorced guys living in the suburbs, at least the age-appropriate ones," Krissa said.

"That's not true, is it?" KC asked.

"Not really. I'm just being jaded and bitter." She held up her phone again. "Here's another common offense: the gym selfie. I will never understand why so many men think the gym selfie is a good idea." She held up a photo of a beefcake in a snug tank top standing next to a rack of weights. His screen name was JackedNHuge."

Daphne studied the photo. "He *is* jacked and huge—you have to give him that."

"And honest, if not exactly modest," KC said. "That's something, right?"

Krissa groaned and tossed the phone into her bag. "So gross. I have dozens more just as awful, but those should give you a general idea of the dating pool I'm dealing with, and how it occasionally leads me to make questionable decisions. You see now why I decided to sleep with real-estate guy?"

"No judgment here," Skylar said.

KC kissed her wedding ring. "Ditto. I'm just impressed that you're making such an effort to meet someone. It sounds exhausting."

"Tell me about it. I swear it takes as much strategic planning as preparing for a trial—and is usually more mentally draining. I can't believe I'm back to the games, the balance between flirting and pretending not to care, the not knowing how long to wait before responding to a text, or what to say in a text, or wondering what *he* means in *his* text, or wondering if you're reading *too much* into his texts, or wondering if you blew it because of a text, or if he even *read* your text. It's enough to drive you crazy! *Then,* on top of all that insanity, once you decide that you *like* a guy, there's the not knowing when to sleep with him for the first time, wondering if he'll lose interest if you do it too soon, or if he'll lose interest if you wait too long. And then if you *do* decide to sleep with him, there's the whole 'Will I regret it?' or 'Will it be any good?' And then what if the sex *isn't* good? Do you give it another chance? Or do you cut and run? And if it *wasn't* good for you, does that mean it wasn't good for him either? It's enough to drive any sane woman over the edge. Your Honor, I rest my case."

Skylar laughed. "That was quite a tirade. I think the jury will be impressed."

"I think that's why I keep seeing Derek," Daphne said. "The alternative seems too daunting."

"What do you mean?" Skylar said. "I thought you were really into him."

Daphne sighed. "I fear that maybe ... I've been lying to myself about that." She realized that she *still* hadn't called him.

*Have I really not given him more than a passing thought all weekend?* Mildly horrified at her behavior, she promised herself she'd call him before leaving for the airport the next day. *He deserves that.*

"I'm sorry, hon," Skylar said, reaching for Daphne's hand and giving it a squeeze. Daphne squeezed back, glad to leave it at that.

"So when do you two head back to whence you came?" Krissa asked Daphne and KC.

"Tomorrow," KC said with a frown. "That makes me sad."

Skylar frowned too. "I can't believe the weekend is already over. It feels like you guys just got here."

"Hey—it's not over *yet*. We still have tonight," Daphne said.

"Should we hit a male strip club?" Krissa asked. "Maybe Hunk-O-Mania?"

"Hunk-O-*what?*" Skylar said.

"Hunk-O-Mania, the all-male dance extravaganza in Midtown. The audience is a virtual melting pot of bachelorette parties from all five boroughs—and New Jersey of course. You've never seen so many sashes, veils, and screaming drunk women in one place."

"Please tell me you're joking," Skylar said.

"I'm not joking about the scene, but I'm *definitely* joking about going. I've been there once, and trust me, once was one time too many."

"Oh thank God. The thought of being in a place like that makes me feel so old," Daphne said.

"Amen to that," Skylar said. "Now, are you ladies ready to head home? I want to make sure KC gets her pregnancy sleep. And by that I mean *I* want to go to bed but am blaming it on the pregnant woman."

"I have no problem with being blamed." KC poked Daphne's side as they stood up. "Up for that run in Central Park we talked about? It'll be fun—a fun run before our last breakfast in New York!"

Skylar coughed. *"Fun run?* What's the term for that, Daphne? You know, when two words that have no business being in the same room are thrown right next to each other?"

"I think the word you're looking for is *oxymoron*," Daphne said.

"Yes. As in I'd be *a moron* to go running with you fitness nuts at the crack of dawn on a holiday when I could be spending that time in my comfortable bed," Skylar said.

"Amen to *that*," Krissa said.

KC ignored them and grinned at Daphne. "What do you think?"

Daphne raised her hand. "As my favorite fitness guru likes to say, I'm in."

# Chapter Twenty-Three

As promised, early the next morning Daphne dragged herself out from under the goose-down comforter and reluctantly changed into workout clothes. Before heading to the kitchen to meet KC, however, she made her way up to the roof deck to call Derek, her internal monologue in tow—and seemingly operating in hyper drive at the thought of speaking with him.

*So much has happened on this trip in, what has it been, only two days? How will I possibly explain it all in a brief phone conversation? How much of it do I want to explain? How much will he want to hear? Besides, he has his boys this weekend and probably won't have much time to chat anyway. Or did he have the boys just Saturday and Sunday?*

She couldn't remember the details—yet another indication that she'd been fooling herself about her feelings for him.

She was about to dial his number, then decided that, given the time difference, it was a bit too early to call, especially on a holiday.

*I'll try him later.*

• • •

Shortly thereafter, Daphne found herself on a brisk run through Central Park with KC, who, despite having taken several weeks off, now seemed determined to prove that being pregnant wouldn't affect her rigorous fitness regimen. Daphne did her best to keep up with her, but as they reached the three-mile mark she began to run out of gas and slowed her pace.

"You okay there, champ?" KC asked.

"Just need to catch my breath. You go on ahead," Daphne said as she slowed to a walk, resting her hands on her hips.

KC began jogging in place ahead of her. "Don't stop now, Daphne! We have only two miles left! You can do it!"

Daphne motioned for KC to keep running. "That's about two miles more than my legs can take right now. I'll walk the rest of the way and meet you back where we started, okay?"

"Are you sure?"

"Positive. Now shoo, I don't want to hold you back."

"Okay, I'll run a little extra then so we can finish around the same time. See you soon!" KC gave Daphne the thumbs-up sign, then turned and dashed ahead, her ponytail bobbing up and down through the back of her baseball cap.

• • •

When she reached the south end of the park, Daphne didn't see KC's pink hat among the people milling about yet, so she made her way to a nearby patch of grass and began to stretch. It wasn't even nine o'clock in the morning, but the world's most popular park was already filling up. The heat rising from the ground told her it was going to be a hot, muggy day, and she was looking forward to a cool shower back at Skylar's before enjoying her last morning in New York City. Soon she'd be back in Columbus, back to her real life, where she'd have to make some important decisions about her future. For now, she just wanted to sit down and enjoy the fresh scent of the grass. She straightened her legs in front of her and leaned into a forward fold, inhaling and exhaling deeply.

Nearly ten minutes later, Daphne saw KC walking toward her in the distance, her hands on her hips. She stood up and waved. "There you are, you track star you. I thought maybe you'd decided to do another full loop."

KC didn't respond, and as she got closer Daphne saw a worried look on her face.

"Hey, are you okay?" Daphne asked.

"I'm not sure. I don't feel so great."

"Morning sickness again?"

"I don't think so. It's not my stomach."

"What is it?"

KC put a hand on her breastbone. "I don't know. I was running pretty fast, and all of a sudden I got this weird feeling right here." She moved her hand a touch to the left.

Daphne's breath hitched. "Your heart?"

KC nodded.

"What does it feel like now? Does it hurt?"

"It's kind of hard to explain. It's not exactly pain, but it just doesn't feel … right."

"What do you mean?"

"I guess maybe *pressure* is the best way to describe it?" KC looked from her chest up at Daphne, and the concern in her eyes turned to fear. "Am I having a heart attack?"

Daphne put an arm around her. "I'm sure you're fine, but we should probably get you checked out just to be safe."

"You mean go to the hospital?"

"Yes."

"I'm scared, Daphne."

"Don't be scared. You're going to be fine. You're the healthiest person I know. You probably just overexerted yourself."

"What if something happens to the baby?" KC whispered. "What if I did something to the baby?"

Daphne squeezed KC's shoulder. "Nothing is going to happen to the baby—or to you. Just try to stay calm, okay? You're going to be fine." She began leading her to the park exit, and with her free hand she pulled her phone out of her pocket and began a search for local hospitals with emergency rooms.

Minutes later, they were in a taxi on their way to Roosevelt Hospital in Midtown West.

# Chapter Twenty-Four

"How is she?" Skylar asked as she took a seat next to Daphne in the waiting room.

"I'm not sure. She's with the doctor now."

"What happened exactly?"

"I wasn't with her, but I guess when she was running her heart started feeling weird."

"Weird how? You mean, like a heart attack?"

Daphne nodded. "They were going to do an EKG and a blood test to see if that's what it was. I guess there are some enzymes that get released into the blood when that happens."

"She can't really have had a heart attack, could she? That's crazy. She's a model of health."

"I know, but the doctor said she wanted to rule it out given the way KC was describing her symptoms."

"You think she overdid it with the running? Is that possible?"

"I don't know. She was going pretty fast, so maybe. She left me in the dust. Or maybe it has something to do with the baby? Maybe something's wrong there? Or maybe something's been wrong all along and it's just now presenting itself?"

Skylar put a hand over her mouth. "It's my fault. She was taking it easy, and I shamed her into working out. What did I call her? A robot?"

"Don't blame yourself, Skylar. If anyone shamed her, *I* did. And besides, her own doctor told her she could exercise."

"I know, but I'm sure it didn't help that I got on her case like that. If she's had a heart attack, I'm never going to forgive myself."

Daphne put a hand on Skylar's shoulder. "Try not to think like that. It's not going to help KC, and it's only going to make us feel worse. I'm going to get a bottle of water from the vending machine. Want anything?"

Skylar looked in the direction of the patient rooms. "No, thanks. I'm going to sit here and wait for the Muppet."

•   •   •

When Daphne returned to the waiting room, Skylar was typing an e-mail into her phone.

"Please tell me you're not working on the Fourth of July weekend, in a *hospital* no less," Daphne said as she took a seat next to her.

"It's not the Fourth of July in China," Skylar said without looking up.

"Good point. What time is it, anyway? I guess we're missing our flights."

"You're definitely missing your flights." She still didn't look up. "No worries, we'll just rebook you for tomorrow."

"At least we'll get to meet James. He gets back from his golfing trip today, right?"

"Unfortunately he's not back until tomorrow night, so it looks like you'll have to wait for the big introduction."

"I hope we get to meet him before the wedding. If not, that would be a little awkward."

Skylar finally looked up from her phone and chuckled. "True. 'Hi, *best friends*, I'd like you to meet my *fiancé*, who momentarily will be *husband*.'"

"By the way, you *do* realize that you have to set a date before there can *be* a wedding ..." Daphne said with a smirk.

"Very funny. And I *will* set a date. I bought a *dress*, remember? And last night I asked Sloane to be a bridesmaid, if she wants to. Or *the* bridesmaid, I should say. I'm sticking to my promise of not subjecting you and KC to that torture."

"That's so sweet of you to ask her! Did she say yes?"

"Yep. I also told her she could wear whatever she wants, even something that's already in her closet. You know how I feel about bridesmaids dresses. I want no part of that scene. I don't really want to deal with choosing a venue either. The flowers, the food, blah blah blah. *Getting* married seems like such a big production when all I really want is to *be* married."

Daphne laughed. "You're like the antibride. I love it. I look forward to the big day, whenever and wherever it turns out to be."

"You'll know as soon as I do. I promise." Skylar checked the time on her phone. "After we get out of here, we can head back to my place and get your flights sorted, then plan a quiet day for KC—depending on how she feels."

"Even if we do absolutely nothing, I love that we get to spend an extra day in New York. Let's just hope everything's all good in there." Daphne's eyes turned toward the examination rooms.

Skylar reached for Daphne's hand and squeezed. "It has to be."

•   •   •

Sometime later, a young female doctor approached Daphne and Skylar. "Hi. I'm Dr. Chan. You're with Ms. Conroy?"

Daphne and Skylar both stood up and shook her hand. "Yes. How is she?" Daphne asked.

"Is she okay?" Skylar added.

Dr. Chan nodded. "She's fine. Her EKG and blood tests both came back negative."

"So that means she didn't have a heart attack?" Daphne asked.

Dr. Chan smiled. "No heart attack."

"Oh, thank God. Then what was it?" Skylar asked.

"Looks like she has a mild case of heartburn."

Skylar laughed. "*Heartburn*? She has a mild case of *heartburn*?"

Dr. Chan gave them an amused-yet-knowing look. "Yes. It's pretty common in pregnancy."

"That's right! I remember getting terrible heartburn when I was pregnant," Daphne said. "I'd completely forgotten about that."

"I had it pretty bad myself a few times with my first-born. It can be scary if you're not familiar with it because it's easy to confuse the discomfort with the symptoms of a heart attack. It's nothing to worry about and is easily treatable," Dr. Chan said.

"You think it could have been triggered by eating a lot of junk food, especially if she doesn't normally eat that sort of thing?" Skylar asked.

"Could be," Dr. Chan said. "Fried food can definitely trigger it."

Skylar chuckled. "I love it. The health nut literally overate herself into the hospital. Where is she?"

Dr. Chan pointed down the hallway. "Room 123, last door on the right. I'm getting her a prescription for an antacid, and then she's free to go."

They made their way to Room 123 and knocked. "Hey woman! You decent? It's us," Skylar said.

"Come in!" KC shouted from behind the closed door.

They entered and found KC changing from the hospital gown back into her shorts and running top.

"So what it is with you ending up in hospitals whenever you're on vacation?" Skylar said. "Didn't we do this exact same thing in Saint Mirika?"

"That's right! The jellyfish sting! I forgot all about that," Daphne said.

KC sat back on the examination table. "I didn't forget. That thing hurt like nobody's business."

Skylar took a seat next to KC. "So … *heartburn?*"

KC covered her face with her hands. "I know! I'm so embarrassed. Totally relieved, but so embarrassed."

"How could you think you were having a heart attack?" Skylar said.

"I've never had heartburn before! And I've never had chest discomfort before! How was I supposed to know the difference? Max is going to die laughing when I tell him. Good thing I didn't have my phone with me when it happened. He would have been so worried for nothing."

"You know, she thought she'd *killed* you," Daphne pointed to Skylar.

KC looked at Skylar. "You thought you'd killed me? Why?"

"Because of the way I called you a robot and heckled you for not exercising. I thought you'd literally run yourself six feet under trying to make up for having sat on your cute little tush for a month."

"I felt horrible too," Daphne said.

KC shook her head. "Please don't feel guilty. Dr. Chan said running had nothing to do with it, although I do think I went a little overboard these last two days. I need to find a happy medium where working out is concerned. Plus, my body just isn't used to indulging like the way I have this weekend. If I'm going to eat for two, I need to find a happy medium there as well."

Skylar clapped her hands. "Well ladies, it looks like you're stuck here for one more day. What do you feel like doing on our last day of the bachelorette weekend?" She put a hand on KC's shoulder. "I never in a million years thought I'd be saying this to *you*, but no more exercise this trip, young lady."

"Or bacon. Or French fries. Or brownies. Or Doritos. Or Swedish Fish," Daphne said.

KC stood up. "I'm up for anything! The only thing on my agenda is to pick up my medicine at the pharmacy. The doctor said she would leave a prescription for me at the front desk."

Skylar coughed. "An *antacid* prescription. I'm going to heckle you about that until the end of time."

KC grinned. "Better antacid than a heart attack, so I'll welcome that heckling."

"So … any ideas on how to spend the rest of your bonus time in New York City?" Skylar looked at both of them as they made their way down the hall. "There are literally a million options, but if either of you has something specific in mind, I'm open to whatever you want to do and wherever you want to go."

"Any*thing* any*where* outside this hospital sounds good to me," KC said.

Daphne, who was walking in front of them, stopped and turned around. "Actually, I do have an idea. Do you have Sloane's number?"

# Chapter Twenty-Five

"You've really never walked across the Brooklyn Bridge?" Daphne said to Skylar as they entered the crowded footpath on the iconic structure that crossed the East River.

"Not that I know much about New York City, but isn't the Brooklyn Bridge like, a major landmark?" KC said.

Skylar shrugged. "Admittedly, it is kind of pathetic that this is my first time, but on the other hand, you know what my travel schedule is like. This is the first weekend I've been in town since April."

"The views up here are even prettier than from the ferry," KC said as she pointed to her right. "Look! There's the Statue of Liberty again! She's still so beautiful!"

"Have you ever been to *Brooklyn* before?" Daphne asked Skylar.

Skylar furrowed her brow in thought. "Once, when I first moved here. It was a long time ago, though. I'm not even sure what part of Brooklyn it was. I was at the early part of the geography learning curve back then."

"What about the other boroughs? What are they again?" KC said.

Skylar held up four fingers, one after the other. "Manhattan, yes, obviously. Queens, no. Staten Island, no. The Bronx, no."

KC pretended to swing a bat. "Three strikes and you're out."

"Guilty as charged," Skylar said.

"The Yankees play in the Bronx, and the Mets play in Queens, right?" KC said.

"You are correct. Maybe we can take in a game on your next trip out here."

When they reached the center of the bridge, Skylar stood on her tiptoes in an effort to peer above the throngs of selfie-taking tourists. "How long is this thing anyway?"

Daphne consulted her phone. "Five thousand, nine hundred, and eighty-nine feet. What is that in miles?"

"A little more than a mile, which is about a mile too long for me. Can we please take a cab back?" Skylar said.

"How about we take the subway?" Daphne said. "It's my and KC's last chance to experience big-city life before we're both back in suburbia."

"Okay, fine," Skylar said.

When they neared the end of the bridge, Daphne pointed to a stairwell ahead of them. "According to the map on my phone, we take that exit. It leads us down into a neighborhood called Dumbo."

"Dumbo actually stands for Down Under the Manhattan Bridge Overpass," Skylar said. "That's the Manhattan Bridge, over there."

Daphne looked at her phone again, then at Skylar. "How did you know that?"

Skylar shrugged. "Hey, just because I don't *go* to Brooklyn doesn't mean I don't *know* about Brooklyn. I'm geographically lazy, not geographically uninformed."

They descended the steps and were soon traversing the cobblestone streets of Dumbo, where grungy coffee houses, mom-and-pop corner bodegas, and dive bars mixed seamlessly with trendy boutiques, luxury apartment buildings, and up-and-coming technology companies. From overhead came the occasional roar of a subway train rolling across the Manhattan Bridge.

"What a delightful neighborhood," Daphne said as they wandered past an art gallery. "It's like a movie set, don't you think? I love the architecture and the peekaboo views of the Manhattan skyline and the East River."

"I dig it too," KC said, her head swiveling to take in the historic converted warehouses and gritty side alleys. "It's so different from what we've seen in Manhattan, but also feels super New Yorky to me."

"New Yorky?" Skylar narrowed her eyes at KC, then looked at Daphne. "Is that a word?"

"I guess it is now." Daphne checked the map on her phone, then pointed left. "According to this, it's two blocks that way. Want to tell Sloane we're almost there?"

"On it. I'm so glad you thought to invite her to join us," Skylar said.

"This is going to be so fun! I haven't been to a flea market in ages. I hope Sloane can help me find something quirky to bring home for Max," KC said. "He loves quirky."

"Obviously," Skylar said. "He married you, didn't he?"

"I already have something in mind for Emma," Daphne said.

"What about Derek?" Skylar asked. "No go?"

Daphne flinched with guilt as she realized she'd never called him. "I don't think so."

"Probably for the best," Skylar said.

KC darted toward the entrance. "Look at this place! It's so ... I can't think of the right word!"

"How about New Yorky?" Skylar called after her.

Daphne and Skylar caught up to KC at the entrance of the dusty, sprawling market known as the Brooklyn Flea. Tucked into a once-abandoned lot just steps away from the East River, it was now a weekend home to dozens of vendors of antique and homemade furniture, wares, and clothing—plus a multitude of culinary entrepreneurs selling everything from kabobs to knishes to kettle corn.

"I'm already starving just *looking* at all those food carts," KC said, her eyes scanning the options.

Skylar pulled a bottle of water out of her purse and handed it to KC. "Easy there, Miss Antacid. We don't want you and that baby you're carrying ending up in the hospital again."

"Boo," KC said with a frown.

"Hey, there's Sloane," Daphne said.

Skylar turned around and waved as Sloane approached them. "Our resident flea market expert is here! Thanks for coming out. I'm so glad you could join us on such short notice."

"Happy to be here. This sounded a lot more fun than studying for my econ midterm, that's for sure," she said with a smile more natural than Daphne had seen on her all weekend.

"Ready to show us around?" Skylar asked.

"I'm ready. Is there anything in particular you were looking for?"

Skylar gestured to Daphne and KC. "Why don't you ask these two lovelies? They are eager to avail you of your services."

"I'd love to find something fun for my husband, like an old clock or something? And maybe a pretty lamp for my bedroom nightstand? I love scented candles too, if they have those here. Or hey, how about something for the baby's room!" KC said.

"I think I can help you with all of the above. What about you, Daphne? Did you have something specific in mind?"

"Actually I do, but before we get started, can Skylar and I make quick stop? Then you can lead the way from there? It will only take a minute. KC, you can come too if you want. But not you, Sloane. It's a surprise."

"Of course. No problem," Sloane said. "Want me to wait for you here?"

"Yes, that would be great. Thanks." Daphne turned on her heel and signaled for Skylar and KC to follow her.

"You're being very mysterious," Skylar said.

"I know. Now follow me. I'm looking for a certain spot."

• • •

Skylar touched Daphne's arm as a small jewelry display in a back area of the market came into view. "Are those what I think they are?" she said.

Daphne smiled. "They are indeed."

"Lokai bracelets! How did you know they would be here?" KC asked.

Daphne pointed to the sign at the top of the booth. "While I was out on my shopping spree the other day, I was hoping to find one for Emma. I did some research on my phone, and this jewelry vendor popped up, along with something about the Brooklyn Flea. I didn't think much about it at the time because I figured we wouldn't get a chance to come over here, but when I found out we had an extra day—and also that Sloane had mentioned she likes going to this market—I thought it would be a fun excursion for all of us to do together." She turned to Skylar. "Plus I thought maybe you'd want to get a bracelet for her."

Skylar picked up a bracelet and ran her fingers over the beads, then hugged Daphne tight. "I *love* that idea. Thank you so much."

"You're welcome. That's what friends are for, right? To think about you when you forget to think about yourself?"

KC leaned in and joined the group embrace. "Can I get in on this action? I think it's what's called a clear bead moment."

# Chapter Twenty-Six

After canvassing the flea market, the quartet—multiple shopping bags in tow—enjoyed a leisurely stroll along the Brooklyn Promenade before joining the long line of patrons snaking into the landmark Brooklyn Ice Cream Factory, situated steps from the East River Ferry docking station and almost directly under the Brooklyn Bridge.

KC wanted a double scoop but reluctantly settled for a single.

"I love the view of Manhattan from here," Daphne said as they all settled onto a bench. The waterfront park faced the East River, with the Brooklyn Bridge to their right and the Statue of Liberty to their left, the famed Wall Street Financial District directly in front of them. "When you're smack in the middle of it, you almost don't realize how beautiful it is."

"Totally," KC said. "What's that saying again? Something about a forest?"

"You mean not being able to see the forest for the trees?" Daphne said.

"Yes! The forest is a clear bead."

Skylar chuckled. "You and those beads."

Sloane held up her new bracelet. "I'm a fan."

"Me too," Daphne said. "I feel like a teenager wearing this thing, but I love it."

Skylar pointed to a skyscraper across the water. "See that skinny building in between those two fat ones? That's my office."

KC squinted "No way!"

"What floor are you on?" Daphne asked.

"Thirty-three."

"That must be quite a view," Sloane said. "I've always wondered what it would be like to work in an office that high."

Skylar turned and looked at her friends and future stepdaughter, all three of them licking their ice cream cones like happy kids on a lazy summer day. "It *is* a nice view, but I like this one better. And trust me, Sloane, you've got plenty of time to work in an office."

"Wise words," KC said. "I wouldn't last two weeks in a cubicle."

"Agreed. I say stay in school for as long as possible," Daphne said.

"See? Smart women, my friends," Skylar said to Sloane. "Hey, want to come over for dinner tonight? Your dad's not back until tomorrow, so it'll be a girls' night in. I'll be making my specialty."

"What's your specialty?" KC asked Skylar. "I didn't think you cooked."

"I don't. My *specialty* is spaghetti noodles and pasta sauce from a jar. That's about all I can manage without burning the place down. James does the cooking in our house."

"Dad does have a special touch in the kitchen. I wish I could join you, but I really need to get studying for that midterm. My plan was to study this afternoon, but I got a little distracted."

"And thank God you did. Otherwise I wouldn't have *these!*" KC polished off the last bit of her ice cream cone, then pulled a blue wall clock painted with white-and-pink daisies out of her shopping bag, along with a tiny antique rattle.

Daphne finished her cone too, then reached for her shopping bag. She pulled out a framed chalk sketch of the Boathouse in Central Park, which Sloane had somehow unearthed in an enormous stack of assorted images. "I know *exactly* where I'm going to put this gem. On the wall in my office." She looked at Sloane. "My *home* office. I don't have a real job."

"Yes, she does. She has an extremely difficult job. She's a *mother*," Skylar said to Sloane. "*And* she's a talented writer. She was at the top of our class in college."

"Along with you." Daphne shot Skylar a grateful look, then turned back to Sloane. "Anyhow, from now on when I get writer's block I'm going to look at that sketch and remember this wonderful trip. I want to come back to New York one day for a book signing. If that doesn't inspire my creative juices and motivate me, nothing will."

"Does that mean you're going to keep working on your novel?" Skylar asked. "Do a rewrite or something?"

Daphne tucked the sketch back into her shopping bag. "Actually … I just started kicking around an idea for a new one."

"Really? Do tell," Skylar said.

Daphne took a breath. "Well … I was joking when I mentioned it yesterday, but now I'm thinking I *could* write a story loosely based on this weekend, you know, about three forty-something friends getting together in New York for a nonbachelorette weekend? Or maybe even a bachelorette weekend? What do you think of that idea?"

"I love it!" KC said. "There's certainly been enough excitement."

"That's for sure," Skylar said. "Comedy, drama, intrigue, romance, even a trip to the ER. I'd say there's enough material in there to fill at *least* a book."

Sloane stopped eating her ice cream cone, a confused look on her face. "Did you say a trip to the ER?"

Skylar pulled KC's ponytail. "We thought this one was dying, but she's fine. I'll fill you in later. Right now I want to hear more about Daphne's new book."

"That's all there really is to tell right now. It's just an idea," Daphne said.

"I think it's a *great* idea. And hey, isn't coming up with the idea the hardest part of anything creative?" KC said. "I think I read that somewhere."

"So you've written a book before?" Sloane said to Daphne. "That's amazing. I've never met a real live author."

Daphne shook her head. "Written, yes. Published, no. Big difference. Technically I'm not an author."

"Stop that. You wrote a damn good book, regardless of what those misguided agents say. So in my eyes, you're an author," Skylar said.

"Thanks, but despite your glowing opinion, after a truckload of rejections it looks like that book isn't going to see the light of day," Daphne said.

"How many is a truckload?" Sloane asked.

"Three dozen."

Sloane's eyes widened. "You got turned down by thirty-six agents?"

"Yep. Number thirty-six was two days ago," Daphne said matter-of-factly.

"Oh wow. I'm so sorry." Sloane said.

"Thanks, but I guess that's kind of the nature of the business. At least I had my friends here to talk me down from the ledge. Anyhow, if I want to get published it looks like my only option might be to try again and see if I can do better the second time around. And now that I have an idea, or at least a partial idea, I'm looking forward to trying again."

"That's the spirit!" KC said.

"It's true. Thanks to you and Skylar, I've remembered how much I enjoy the act of writing. Not just putting the words on the page, but thinking about the story behind them, the whole creative process I guess. I shouldn't lose sight of that, regardless of the end product. So maybe this next effort will be a short story, or maybe a full book, or maybe just a bunch of journal entries that won't earn me a dime, but the most important thing is that I think I'll have fun writing it, whatever form *it* takes. I guess when it comes down to it, that's the most important thing."

KC was about to say something when Skylar covered her mouth. "I know, I know. The beads," Skylar said.

"Clr bds!" KC tried to shout through Skylar's hand.

"So anyhow, that's the idea. Or maybe it's better to call it the seedling of an idea. I have no clue how it would end, for example."

"What, you mean having you and KC ride off into the sunset that is JFK airport wouldn't be enough?" Skylar said.

Daphne pursed her lips. "I feel like something more dramatic than that would need to happen. Not that you guys *aren't* interesting, but you know what I mean."

Skylar nudged her arm. "I'm sure you'll come up with something. I have faith in that imagination of yours."

"I'm impressed you have the courage to write another book after being turned down like that," Sloane said. "I don't know if I'd be able to start all over and risk being rejected again. To feel that disappointment again."

Skylar turned to face Sloane. "Actually, I believe a fresh start is *exactly* what you need. I still think you should consider transferring, if not to NYU then maybe to somewhere outside the city. We weren't joking when we said you should postpone the real world for as long as possible. Not that the real world can't be fun, but there's nothing quite like those college years."

"This may be a dumb question, but have you ever thought about Northwestern?" KC peered around Skylar and asked Sloane.

Sloane looked at her hands. "Actually yes, a little bit."

"Really?" Skylar asked.

*Maria Murnane*

Sloane nodded. "You talk so highly about it, and then after seeing the three of you together this weekend, and how close you still are after all these years—how could I not?"

Skylar didn't say anything. Instead she put an arm around Sloane, pulling her close.

"Hey, I have an idea," Daphne said. "Why don't Emma and I meet you two there for a joint campus visit?"

"Emma?" Sloane said.

"My daughter. She'll be a senior in high school this fall."

"I think I'd like that," Sloane said.

Skylar gave Daphne a puzzled look. "I thought you wanted Emma to go to Ohio State so she'd be close to home."

"I do, but now I realize that her choice shouldn't be about what's best for me, it should be about what's best for her. And maybe that means leaving Columbus."

"Maybe you should think about that for yourself," Skylar said.

Daphne looked at her, then felt her lips curl up into a tiny smile. "Maybe I should."

KC raised a hand. "A trip back to Evanston sounds so fun! Can I come too?"

Skylar grabbed KC's fingers. "Do you know who you look like when you do that?"

KC shook her head.

"Her." Skylar stood up, pulling KC with her, then pointed with her free hand across the river ... toward the Statue of Liberty.

KC grinned. "I'll take that comparison any day. Here's to girl power!"

•   •   •

On the walk back to Skylar's apartment from the Chambers Street subway stop, Daphne's phone chimed with a text. She froze when she saw that it was from Clay.

*Hi Daphne, good to hear from you! Sorry for the late reply, was away for the holiday. I'd love to see you if you're still in town. Maybe a drink later this afternoon? LMK*

"Oh my God," Daphne said.

"Everything okay, sweets?" Skylar asked.

Daphne held up her phone. "I just got a text from Clay Handsome."

*"What?"* KC said.

Skylar narrowed her eyes. "He just *happened* to text you?"

Daphne blushed. "Okay, busted. I texted him on Saturday, you know, after I'd had all that champagne? I didn't tell you guys because I felt a little silly, to be honest. And then when he didn't reply within a few hours, I forgot all about it."

"Fair enough. What does the text say?" Skylar asked.

"He wants to get together. What does LMK mean?"

"Let me know," KC said.

"How do you know that?" Daphne asked.

"Josh and Jared use it all the time."

Daphne sighed. "Great. I'm too old to understand his texts. I can't meet up with him if I'm too old to understand his texts!"

"Stop it. You're *not* too old, and he wouldn't have asked you to meet up if he didn't want to see you," Skylar said. "No one's *that* polite."

"So you think I should do it?"

"Of course you should. Why wouldn't you?" Skylar said. "It's not like you're in a committed relationship, right?"

"Definitely not," Daphne said.

"Seeing him would be a good side plot for your new book," KC said. "You know, add a little spice?"

Daphne laughed. "It would be fun to add a little spice."

"Do it!" Skylar said. "When does he want to meet?"

"This afternoon."

"Perfect. Prego here can take a snooze, and I can use the time to catch up on work."

Daphne bit her lip, already nervous. "Okay, I'll do it."

# Chapter Twenty-Seven

As she approached Lumos on Houston Street later that afternoon, Daphne smoothed her hands over her new pink dress—the one thing she'd kept from her shopping spree.

*I'm getting my money's worth out of it, that's for sure.*

She glanced at a window to evaluate her appearance. Skylar had helped with her hair as well as her makeup, so at least she looked decent. She stopped at the entrance, took a deep breath, then reached for the door and pulled it open. She'd wondered if the place would be a frat-guy type dive bar and was relieved to see it was nothing of the sort. A long, narrow space, Lumos was quiet and cozy and quite grown-up, with dark hardwood floors and a wall of exposed brick facing the bar.

The place was almost empty, so she spotted Clay immediately. He was sitting on a bar stool, typing into his phone.

*God, he's still so good-looking*, she thought.

Tall, with broad shoulders and thick, wavy brown hair. His green eyes were accentuated by the mint-colored button-down he had on with khaki shorts and flip-flops.

*Clay Handsome* is *the perfect nickname for him.* She had to hand it to Skylar. *So spot-on with those monikers.*

She approached and tapped him gently on the shoulder. "Hi, stranger."

"Daphne, hi! Sorry, hang on for half a sec." He sent off the text he'd been composing, then stood up and gave her a bear hug so strong it almost lifted her off her feet. "It's so good to see you. Did you have any trouble finding the place?"

"None at all. I actually walked here from my friend's apartment and didn't get lost once. I almost feel like a real New Yorker now. I even know that this street is pronounced *Howston*, not *Hewston*."

"Well done. You're one of us now. You look amazing, by the way. Just as beautiful as I remember."

Daphne felt her nerves jump at the compliment. "Thanks. You look quite handsome yourself, very sun-kissed. That's not from rollerblading by any chance, is it?"

"Never been rollerblading, but I did get some sun at the beach this weekend. I guess I got a little fried. I always *think* about putting on sunscreen, but when it comes to actually *putting on* sunscreen, it's like there's this big disconnect that I just can't bridge."

"Well, it suits you just fine. I asked about roller-blading because I saw your doppelganger fly by me in Tribeca the other day."

Clay patted the stool next to him. "Please, have a seat. I hope my doppelganger didn't crash and break an arm or anything. That would be just my luck—for him to make a fool of himself in front of you."

Daphne laughed. "Nope, he had great form from what I could tell. Like an Olympic speed skater on pavement."

"Glad to hear that. Now, what can I get you to drink?"

She glanced at the glass of water on the counter in front of him and was impressed that he'd waited for her to arrive before ordering. He was still such a gentleman. "What are you going to have?"

"Chardonnay. I know that sounds a little girly, but I love a chilled chardonnay on a hot day."

"I do too. So refreshing, right? I'd love some water as well, thanks."

The bartender poured their drinks, and Clay lifted his glass to Daphne's for a cheers. "Here's to once-new friends who are now old friends."

"Are we old friends now?"

"I guess so, but we probably fall somewhere on the spectrum of more than friends," he said with a chuckle.

Daphne smiled and took a sip of her wine.

*We were more than friends in Saint Mirika, that's for sure.*

"So what brings you to town?"

"Do you remember my friend Skylar?"

"Skylar … hmm. Help me out? I used to be great with names, but ever since I turned thirty I can't seem to remember my own."

Daphne playfully pushed his shoulder. "Yeah, right. You're *so* over the hill now. Thirty! You'll be using a walker soon."

He laughed. "So Skylar is …"

"The pretty redhead? Kind of no-nonsense?"

"Ah yes! She's the one who didn't play flag football with us. What was the name of your friend with the rocket arm again?"

"KC."

"KC! I remember now. That girl could throw a football like a college quarterback. So you were saying ... Skylar?"

"She's engaged now, so we're here to celebrate."

"Ah! A bachelorette weekend."

"Yes, a bachelorette weekend. Although it's been pretty tame." She figured there was no reason to go into the shifting nomenclature they'd used.

"So when's the big date?"

"For the wedding? They haven't set one yet."

"Are you the maid of honor?"

"She's not having one. She's not going to have any bridesmaids, except I think maybe her fiancé's daughter."

"So no big, poofy dress for you?"

Daphne laughed. "No big, poofy dress for me, thank God."

"That's too bad. It's always kind of funny to see those poor women wearing those things. Some of them are truly frightening." He set his glass down. "So how *are you*, Daphne? What's new in—where do you live again? Chicago?"

"Columbus."

He snapped his fingers. "That's right. Columbus. But you went to school in Chicago. Northwestern Wildcats— love their purple, love their marshmallows. It's all coming back to me now."

"Good memory. And you went to Michigan. Just as cold, better football team."

"Ah, so you have a good memory too."

"I guess I do." She tried not to stare at him, but it wasn't easy. He was as attractive as she remembered, maybe even more so now, and she suddenly felt an urge to kiss him.

*Would it be nuts if I leaned over and planted one on him?* She balled her hand into a fist. *That's ridiculous. We're in New York, not Saint Mirika. That was then, and this is now. I'm not going to kiss him.*

But she couldn't help wanting to kiss him.

*Maybe he'll kiss me?*

She buried her nose in her wine glass and hoped he couldn't read her thoughts.

"So why didn't you ever get in touch, Daphne?"

She looked up. "What?"

He chuckled. "After Saint Mirika. I thought you'd at least text to say hi or *something.*"

"You did?"

"Of course I did. I would have texted you, but I didn't have your number."

She felt her cheeks flush. "Oh, I'm sorry. I ... um ... I guess I thought you wouldn't want to hear from me. You know, what happens in Saint Mirika stays in Saint Mirika?" She gave him an awkward smile and suddenly felt like a sophomore in high school.

He chuckled again. "Okay, I get it. No harm, no foul. And definitely no hard feelings. But hey, I'm really glad you reached out now. It's great to see you again."

"It's great to see you too."

*God, I want to kiss him.*

"So what have you been up to since I last saw you?" he asked.

Daphne sat up a little straighter, finally comfortable with how to answer the question. "Well, I wrote a novel, actually."

"You did? That's incredible! Congratulations."

She cleared her throat. "Thanks, but there's more to the story. I wrote a novel, or I guess I should say a manuscript, but unfortunately it looks like I'm not going to get it published. So I think I'm going to write another one. A better one, I hope."

"I'm sorry to hear that, but good for you for keeping your chin up and having another go at it. For what it's worth, I hear it's almost impossible to get a book published, especially the first time around."

"I'm learning that. I just wish I had known that before I wrote mine."

"You wouldn't have written it, then?"

"I think I would have, actually I *know* I would have, but being more informed about how slim my chances were would have prepared me to handle the flood of rejections I got much better than I did. I probably wouldn't have said that a few days ago because I was feeling so sorry for myself, but spending time with my friends this weekend has made me remember how much I enjoyed *writing* the book. It's the *creating* part that's most important, not necessarily the *getting published* part. I forgot that for a while there."

"I like your attitude, Daphne."

"Thanks. It's feeling kinda new to me—but I like it too."

"I bet a lot of successful authors do that. You know, write a book and stick it in a drawer, then write another one using what they learned writing the first one, and it's the second effort that cracks open the door. Maybe that will happen to you."

"That would be fantastic, but I'm not counting my chickens."

"What's the book about, anyway?"

"Oh, it's probably not up your alley. It's more for a female audience. About life challenges and friendship and that sort of thing."

If it wasn't going to see the light of day she didn't see the need to tell him that he'd inspired a character, even though she knew he'd probably be flattered.

"And the next one?"

"Actually, I'm thinking of basing it on this trip to New York."

"Really? So I'll get to be in it?"

She gave him a flirtatious smirk. "Maybe. I guess we'll see."

*A steamy make-out session would be fun to write about, that's for sure.*

Just thinking about it made her insides stir. She wondered what he'd do if he knew what was running through her head right now.

He held up his glass for another toast. "Well, here's wishing you the best of luck. I've never met a published author before, so I hope you will be the first."

She clinked her glass against his. "Thanks, Clay. You're a real sweetheart. So what about you? What have you been up to since Saint Mirika?" As she sipped her drink she looked at the dimple on his left cheek and imagined her protagonist caressing it in her new book.

*Then he'd take her by the hand and lead her into the bedroom ...*

He grinned and set his glass on the bar. "A lot, actually. It's funny that you're here for a bachelorette weekend, because ... Well, because I recently got engaged too."

Daphne coughed so hard that she almost spit out her wine.

"Are you okay?" Clay asked.

She pounded her chest and reached for her water. "Yep, I'm fine. Just went down the wrong pipe."

*That's a complete lie, but what am I supposed to say? That I've been fantasizing about making out with him in broad daylight in a public place? That I'm probably going to write a sexy scene about him in the book I'm going to start the moment I get back to Columbus? Actually, writing something just like this in my new book would be pretty funny. Would the reader see it coming? I certainly didn't.*

She drank some more water and forced a smile. "You're really engaged? Wow! That's wonderful."

"Yep. Can you believe it? After all those expensive bachelor weekends I complained to you about going to, now *I'm* the guy my buddies will be bitching about. I guess I deserve it, given how much grief I gave them."

Then it hit her.

*His sunburn.*

"Were you on your bachelor party *this weekend?*"

He shook his head. "Just the beach. My fiancée, Ariel, and I headed to the Hamptons. Her parents have a place out there."

"Ah, the Hamptons. Sounds lovely."

She made a mental note to tell Krissa that her theory about single men and their beach vacations had just been bolstered. Then she had another thought.

*I should put that theory into my next book too!*

She felt energized by the ideas popping into her head and wished she'd brought a notebook to jot them down. Then, out of nowhere, she blurted out, "I'm headed to a lake house with my boyfriend in a couple weeks. Not quite the Hamptons, but should be fun."

She flinched. *Where had* that *declaration come from?*

"You have a boyfriend? That's great, Daphne, although not surprising. I figured you'd have been snatched up by now. What's his name?"

"Derek."

"Well, Derek is a lucky guy. I'm happy for you."

"Thanks. I'm happy too."

*Why am I lying like this? If anything, seeing Clay has made it crystal clear that I'm not feeling it, whatever it is, for Derek.*

They continued chatting for a half hour or so, then together stepped out of the bar and into the bright afternoon sunlight.

"Well, I guess this is goodbye," Clay said.

"I guess so," Daphne said.

He wrapped her in another bear hug and kissed the top of her head. "Take care of yourself, Daphne. You deserve the best," he whispered.

As they went their separate ways, Daphne knew that this time it would be for good.

# Chapter Twenty-Eight

On the walk back to Skylar's apartment, Daphne couldn't help but laugh at herself. She didn't think Clay had any idea what had been running through her mind during their time together, but *she* knew what she'd been thinking, and she felt silly for it. She was happy for him, though. He was a nice person, and she wished him well in his marriage.

She was disappointed in herself, however, for again having overstated the seriousness of her relationship with Derek.

*It was a knee-jerk reaction, but why had it happened in the first place? Do I really believe that Clay, Skylar, KC, or anyone, for that matter, would think less of me if I simply stated the truth? That I've been seeing someone but don't think it's going to work out? What's so wrong with being single again? Or at all?*

She looked around the sidewalk at all the happy couples strolling hand in hand and wondered if everlasting love—the kind of intense, unbreakable connection that would make her believe *I belong with this person*—was in her future.

Was there a secret formula for finding someone to love who would love you in return? Or, as Krissa had said, did it just come down to luck? And to timing?

*It sure does seem like finding love is about as easy as finding a needle in a haystack—and even then there's no guarantee that it won't prick you down the road.*

She thought of Krissa and the effort she was making to meet someone special, and how it had led only to disappointment after disappointment. Daphne didn't think she could stomach that. Not that she'd tried very hard herself to meet someone new. She hadn't tried at all, really.

*And then Derek had called, and it was nice. He is nice. It isn't fireworks, but it's* nice.

*Nice isn't enough, though. For either of us.*

She stopped walking and looked back in the direction of the bar, thinking of the sparks she'd just felt with Clay. The banter, the teasing, the effortless conversation about things both playful and important—all of it happening with an accelerated heart rate. *That* was the kind of connection she wanted.

*I could keep telling myself that I have my foot on the brake with Derek for fear of getting hurt again, but I know that's not the truth. I do want to find love again. I just haven't wanted to admit to myself that I'm never going to find it with him. Maybe it's impractical to hold out for that flutter of excitement, to wait for the real deal, but I've been practical for too long now. I'm not going to settle.*

*It's time to rip off the Band-Aid and tell Derek it's over.*

She pulled out her phone to call him, then quickly reconsidered.

*He deserves better than a call from a noisy street corner. I should wait until I'm back at Skylar's.*

But given how much she suddenly wanted to give him the news, she knew she had made the right decision.

•    •    •

When the elevator door opened to Skylar's apartment, the place was as quiet as a mouse. KC and Skylar were most likely napping, Daphne figured. The battery on her phone was nearly dead, so she decided to use the landline in the living room to call Derek instead of heading downstairs for her charger and risk waking her friends up. She stretched out on one of the recliner chairs and put her feet up on an ottoman, then dialed his number. A tiny part of her hoped he wouldn't pick up, but he answered on the second ring.

"Hello?"

"Hey there."

"Who is this?"

"It's Daphne."

"Daphne? Did you get a new phone?"

"Oh no, sorry. I'm using my friend's landline in New York. I'm *so* sorry I haven't called earlier. I meant to, but you know how crazy things can get when you're with friends." She hated how lame that sounded. She was definitely not good at this.

"No problem. I get it. So you've had a good time, then?" His tone was one of surprise, as if he hadn't expected to hear from her.

*Maybe he already knows what's coming?*

"Yes. A fantastic time, actually. We've had a couple hiccups, but I guess hiccups make for good stories, right? What about you? How was your weekend?" She knew she needed to get to the point, but she couldn't bring herself to do it.

*Why does he have to be so nice?*

"It was good. Listen, now's not a really good time. Can we talk tomorrow?"

His voice sounded a little muffled.

Daphne hesitated. Something was off, but she didn't know what it was. It was almost as if she'd caught him at a bad time at the office, but today was a holiday.

Then her woman's intuition kicked in, and the reason he sounded strange suddenly dawned on her.

*He's not alone.*

"Are you with someone else right now?" she asked. She clearly didn't mean his kids.

Silence.

"Are you with … a woman?"

"Daphne, listen—"

"Someone you're dating?"

"Yes. I'm sorry for not being more up front about that."

She coughed out a laugh. "No! It's fine. No explanation needed, really. I understand."

*So that was why he needed an answer about the lake house by today—so he could invite someone else if I said no? Am I even the first woman he invited? Hell, for all I know, he's dating half of Chicago. And why shouldn't he? He's a fantastic guy who's been through a rough divorce. He deserves to have fun and be happy—and maybe even find someone to love.*

226

*Just like I deserve. Just like Krissa deserves. Just like everyone deserves.*

Daphne thought of the framed picture of Skylar and James and knew she and Derek would never have that kind of chemistry. There was absolutely nothing wrong with him, but she knew in her gut that he just wasn't for her. But that didn't mean he wouldn't be a perfect fit for someone else.

Derek's voice yanked her back to the conversation. "I'm really sorry, Daphne. I didn't mean for this to happen, at least like this. Can we talk about it later?" His tone was notably strained with guilt. "This is kind of a bad time."

She smiled into the phone and felt an emotional weight lift from somewhere inside her.

"Sure, I'd like that. I think we both know we're probably better off just as friends anyway, so why don't we skip the lake house, okay?"

"You're sure you're not upset?"

"Not at all."

"I'm sorry, Daphne."

"Please, Derek. It's okay. I completely understand."

And she did.

# Chapter Twenty-Nine

Later that evening Skylar, Daphne, and KC sat down to a simple pasta dinner on one end of Skylar's handcrafted dining room table—which had seating for twelve.

"So Clay Handsome's engaged, and you and Chicago Derek are officially no longer. I take a nap for like forty-five minutes and all hell breaks loose," Skylar said.

Daphne laughed. "I think you're being a little dramatic. But it *was* an eventful afternoon."

"You think Derek's been seeing other people all along?" KC asked.

"I have no idea. Probably. Serves me right for making assumptions. The truth was, we never actually defined *what* our relationship was, much less talked about where it was going. I got myself so worked up over my own ambivalence, over my own guilt about feeling more friendship than romance, that it had never occurred to me that he might be experiencing similar doubts."

"So it's for the best, then?" KC added.

"Definitely. We weren't right for each other. And as for seeing Clay again, well that was more for fun anyway—even though I did kind of want to jump into his lap at the bar."

"You could always do that in your book," Skylar said with a shrug.

Daphne laughed. "I was thinking the same thing! I guess I know how that plot thread will wrap up, plus the one with the Derek character too. Now if only I could figure out how to end the *main* part of the story. Right now in my head it's just a big black dot."

"Something will come to you, I'm not worried. Just promise me you'll write it," Skylar said.

"I will. I promise."

Maybe the book she'd already written wasn't ready to be taken to the next level—but hey, it was her first try. That didn't mean she couldn't write another story, a better story, one that *was* ready. She realized now that when Emma left for school next year she would be okay by herself. She'd be more than okay, because she had her writing to fulfill her now. Maybe in the future, perhaps even the near future, she'd be motivated to make the kind of effort that Krissa was making to find someone special, or maybe Lady Luck would smile down on her and she'd stumble into it without lifting a finger. But right now she wasn't worried about that. Right now what she really wanted to do was to sit down at her desk and get to work on her second novel. She knew she was a good writer, and she wasn't giving up. She had the solid foundation for a story now—everything but the ending. Her mind began to drift as she thought of various possibilities, though nothing seemed quite right.

*Maybe I'll just have to see how the real weekend turns out first. It's not over yet.*

Just then, they heard the elevator door open.

"Were you expecting someone?" Daphne asked Skylar.

Skylar looked confused. "Not that I know of. Maybe Sloane decided to come by after all?"

"Maybe it's Krissa with more dating stories!" KC said.

A deep voice boomed through the apartment. "Hey babe! You home?"

"It's James!" Skylar jumped up and darted toward the elevator.

"That's the fastest I've ever seen her move," Daphne said.

KC laughed. "No kidding."

A moment later, a beaming Skylar approached the dining room table arm in arm with a smiling James. Like his daughter, he was tall and lanky with striking green eyes.

"Ladies, this is James," Skylar said. "James, this is Daphne and KC."

James greeted each of them with a friendly hug. "What a pleasure to finally meet you both. Since you three planned this trip, Skylar's talked of little else."

"Likewise," KC said. "I've been wanting to meet the lucky fellow who finally stole our girl's heart."

Daphne nodded. "As you can imagine, they've been lining up for decades in pursuit, but until she met you they'd all been turned away empty-handed."

James laughed. "Oh, believe me, I know I must have done something pretty special in a previous life to be so fortunate in this one."

"Maybe you ran an orphanage, or you rescued a bunch of kittens and puppies from a burning building," KC said.

"I'm thinking I figured out a way to stop people from honking in traffic. Anyone who can do *that* deserves eternal happiness."

Skylar laughed and kissed him on the cheek. "You're too sweet, sweets. Welcome home. I thought you weren't coming back until tomorrow?"

"I wasn't going to, but when you told me your friends were staying an extra night, I decided to cut my trip short. Who knows when they might be back in town?"

"You really did that?" Skylar said.

"Of course. I can lose badly to Patrick on the links any day of the week. But how often do I get a chance to meet your best friends and see the infamous Three Musketeers in action? Plus I missed you, obviously."

Skylar gestured toward the ceramic bowls of spaghetti and mixed green salad on the table. "Well, the weekend has been filled with adventure, but I fear we're being decidedly underwhelming at the moment. After this world-class meal we were going to watch a movie and eat popcorn. You still glad you came back early?"

"You *cooked?* Now I *know* it's a special occasion. This calls for the good wine. Hang on, I'll be back in a flash." He turned on his heel and headed into the kitchen.

As soon as he was out of sight, Skylar turned to face Daphne and KC, a dreamy smile on her face. "Isn't he great?"

"I love him!" KC shouted.

"I love you too!" James shouted back.

KC covered her mouth with her hand. "Oops, sorry," she whispered.

Skylar laughed as she took a seat at the table. "It's okay, he deserves some props after what he just did. I can't believe he came back from his golf trip a day early just to meet you two."

"I can," KC said. "He loves *you*, and you love *us*, so by applying the transitive property to emotions, he loves us too—though not in the *love* love sense, of course."

Daphne looked blankly at her. "I have no idea what any of that means."

Skylar turned to Daphne and lowered her voice. "So this may sound a little crazy, but I think I just came up with an idea for how to end your new book."

"Really? What is it?"

Skylar kept her voice hushed. "Well, I was thinking that maybe you'd be interested in having your art, as they say, imitate life."

"How so?" Daphne asked.

Skylar stole a glance at the kitchen. "Would you two be up for staying in town a few more days?"

# Chapter Thirty

Skylar squeezed Daphne and KC's hands as the town car inched through the afternoon traffic. "Am I really about to do this?"

Daphne squeezed back. "You bet you are."

The car pulled to a stop, and Daphne opened the door and stepped outside into the afternoon sunshine, then turned to help Skylar. "Be careful with the train," she said.

Skylar climbed out of the car and onto the sidewalk, with KC following close behind. A steady stream of passersby glanced approvingly in Skylar's direction.

"I feel kind of silly in this thing," Skylar said as the car pulled away from the curb.

"What are you talking about? You look gorgeous!" KC said.

"I'm still amazed that we were able to get it altered in one day. I was afraid that might be the glitch in your plan," Daphne said.

"That's the beauty of New York," Skylar said. "If you're willing to pay for it, you can basically live a glitch-free existence."

KC pointed to the entrance. "Speaking of which, let's get you hitched without a glitch."

"Look who's a poet," Skylar said.

As they made their way toward the front steps of the building, Daphne looked to her left. "Hey, there's Krissa!"

The three of them waited for Krissa to emerge from the crowd of pedestrians. "Hi lovely." Skylar kissed her on the cheek.

Krissa whistled. "Holy hell, Skylar. You look amazing."

Skylar smoothed her dress. "You don't think it's a little much for city hall?"

"Who cares? It's your wedding day, and you look hot, and that's the end of it. Your Honor, I rest my case."

"Thanks babe. And thanks for coming. I know it's not easy to escape from that office of yours," Skylar said.

"True, but not even the top partner himself could stop me from being here, although I did get a few curious looks when I said I was leaving at three o'clock on a Wednesday to go to a wedding. Sorry I couldn't meet up with you and your besties earlier to help you get ready and all that fun stuff. You two look great, by the way."

"Thanks! So do you," Daphne said. "Professional, yet stylish."

Krissa looked down at her tailored suit. "My boring law-firm uniform, you mean? I have it in black, navy, gray, and brown. Shoot me now. As you can see, Wednesday is navy day."

"Just four colors for five days?" KC said.

"Casual Fridays. Or I should say *business* casual, so equally boring. Can you see why I go a little wild child on the weekends? I need to get the corporate slave out of my system."

KC's eyes lit up. "Got any more stories for us?"

"I wish I could regale you with more ridiculousness, but alas I've been doing nothing but conducting soul-killing depositions in a poorly lit conference room this week." Krissa patted KC's shoulder, then turned to Daphne. "If your daughter ever considers going to law school, I highly recommend you lock her in a closet until she comes to her senses."

Daphne laughed. "I'll remember that."

"So how's the extended trip been? It's like you two live here now."

"We've had *so* much fun," Daphne said. "On Monday we walked across the Brooklyn Bridge and went to the Brooklyn Flea, then yesterday while Skylar and James went to pick up their marriage license and Skylar got her dress fitted, KC and I went shopping for something to wear today. Then, when they got back, they took us to lunch in Bryant Park. Then we all went to the Empire State Building and Times Square before they treated us to a delicious dinner at an Italian place near their apartment—after which we had a glass of wine on the roof deck. I'm going to miss that roof deck."

"Don't forget we went to the Tenement Museum too," Skylar said.

"I loved the Tenement Museum!" KC said. "Is that rude to say? If feels kind of rude to say I enjoyed seeing what a tenement looks like."

"They were tenements like a hundred years ago. I think you're fine," Skylar said.

Krissa turned to Skylar. "You did all that in one day? Who are you, and what have you done with Skylar?"

"I know, right? It's like once I embraced my inner tourist, she took on a life of her own. I think I've done more sightseeing in the past few days than I have in all the years I've lived here."

KC took a step backward and craned her neck at the soaring white pillars of city hall. "This is such a pretty building."

Skylar elbowed her. "Kind of New Yorky, don't you think?"

"Yes, very New Yorky!"

"Say what?" Krissa said.

"Just go with it," Daphne said.

"You're looking kind of New Yorky yourself," Skylar said to KC. "I can't believe you're wearing a dress again. A *girly* one, no less. What's gotten into you? Oh wait, a *fetus*."

"Doesn't she look pretty?" Daphne said. "We found it at one of those boutiques near your apartment. Just don't call it a bridesmaid dress."

Skylar held up her hands. "Hey, if anyone bought a bridesmaid dress, don't pin it on me. I like your little number as well, by the way," she said to Daphne. "Very flattering cut."

Daphne did a little curtsey and modeled her forest-green shift dress. "Why thank you. This one is *not* from one of those cute boutiques near your apartment." True to her commitment to staying within her budget, she'd bought it at Century 21 in the Financial District, which to her delight was like a TJ Maxx, Ross, and Marshalls all rolled into one enormous discount store.

KC tugged at the strap of her dress. "Mine's kind of itchy."

"Nonbridesmaids don't get to complain about their dresses," Skylar said.

"That reminds me—where's Sloane?" Daphne asked.

"She was coming with her dad, so she's probably already inside," Skylar said.

Krissa checked her watch and looked at the entrance. "Speaking of which, I hate to bust up the flash mob sidewalk party, but methinks there's a handsome man in there waiting for a certain someone to do a certain something."

KC did a little dance. "Skylar's getting married! Skylar's getting married!"

Daphne stepped in front of Skylar and put both hands on her shoulders. "You ready to do this?"

Skylar closed her eyes and took a deep breath, then slowly exhaled as she opened them. "I think so."

"Come on now, you can do better than that!" KC said.

Krissa laughed. "Seriously. Throw your fans a bone here."

Skylar laughed too. "You're right. That was pretty lame. Sorry, I'm just a little nervous."

"Understandable," Krissa said. "You're only pledging your eternal love and devotion to another human being. No biggie."

Daphne squeezed Skylar's hand. "You're okay, right?"

Skylar squeezed back. "I'm okay."

"Ask her again, Daph," KC said.

Daphne returned her hands to Skylar's shoulders. "Are you ready to get married?"

Again Skylar closed her eyes and took a deep breath, but this time when she opened them, they were filled with tears. Her face broke into a smile—a wide, beaming expression that said the word for her, but she said it anyway. "Yes."

Then she added, "Bring it on."

•   •   •

Later, in the West Village, the newly married couple's celebratory dinner took place in a cozy back corner of the Waverly Inn. The guest list consisted of KC, Daphne, Krissa, James's golf buddy Patrick and his wife, Erika, their college-age nephew, Christopher, and Sloane, who was a vision of youthful elegance in a sleeveless black cocktail dress. She wore a long strand of pearls around her neck, but her wrist was adorned with her new Lokai bracelet.

Both ends of the table buzzed with lively conversation. As Daphne made small talk at one end with boyishly handsome Christopher, she caught him staring at Sloane—seated on the far end, next to Krissa—more than once. After the third time, she discreetly motioned for Sloane to come sit in the empty seat next to her. It took a few moments, but Sloane finally made her way over.

"Sloane, did you know that Christopher goes to Penn?" Daphne casually asked as she joined them.

Sloane looked at Christopher with a shy smile. "Really? What are you majoring in?" Daphne was proud of her. She could tell she was nervous but was doing her best not to come across as cold.

Christopher was clearly nervous too, as he swallowed before answering. "I'm studying finance, so I'm interning this summer at my aunt's advisory firm here in Manhattan."

"Oh, that sounds interesting," Sloane said. Then she looked at her hands, evidently unsure what to say next.

Daphne remembered how little contact she'd had with boys her own age. *The poor thing.*

Sloane's battered self-esteem belied her beauty and grace.

"Yeah. I mean, it's only been a week, but I like it so far," Christopher said. "Where do you go?"

"Columbia. I'm majoring in econ."

"Oh, cool."

An awkward pause followed, and Daphne was glad she was no longer that age. Flawless skin was not worth the social angst. After one too many seconds of silence, she decided to nudge things along. "Penn's in Philadelphia, right, Christopher?" She didn't want to push *too* hard, but it was obvious they could both use a little help to get a conversation going.

Christopher smiled. "Yes."

Sloane nodded and smiled as well, but didn't speak.

After another prolonged silence, Daphne chose to be a bit more direct. "I hear that's a great school. And Philadelphia's not *too far* from New York, right Sloane?"

She looked determinedly at the young woman to make it clear what she was getting at.

Then it clicked. Sloane thanked Daphne with her eyes before answering. "It's about two hours by train." Then she turned to Christopher. "Do you like it there? I'm actually thinking of transferring schools."

"You are? That's cool. Yeah, I really like it there. I mean, it was a little hard at first because I didn't know anyone and kind of missed high school, but once I made some friends it really started to grow on me, you know what I mean? And now I can't imagine being anywhere else."

Sloane gestured in Skylar's direction. "Maybe I should check it out. Skylar, I mean my stepmom, and I are already planning to go look at Northwestern, and probably some other schools too." She glanced briefly at Daphne, then regained eye contact with Christopher. "If we come for a visit, maybe you could show us around campus?"

*Success!* Daphne thought.

Christopher looked thrilled. "For sure. And maybe you could show me around New York while I'm here? I don't know anyone here except my aunt and uncle."

"I'd be happy to. I got a little taste of playing tour guide this weekend with Daphne and KC, and it sounds like my stepmom took them all over the place. Maybe we could follow in their footsteps?"

"Sounds like a plan," Christopher said with a grin.

"Be careful what you wish for. Skylar ran us *ragged*," Daphne said as she stood up and tucked her chair against the table.

Sloane and Christopher both laughed, and at the sound of her name Skylar glanced up and made eye contact with Daphne, who discreetly tilted her head as she made her way toward Sloane's former seat.

Skylar looked over at Sloane and Christopher, chatting like they were old friends, then back at Daphne and winked.

●   ●   ●

After the entrées had been served and the champagne had been poured, Daphne tapped her fork against her water glass. The din of chatter at the table quieted down, and she stood up.

Krissa lifted her champagne flute. "I sense a toast is upon us. Let's hear it!"

Daphne took a sip of water, then cleared her throat and looked at Skylar. "When I came to New York a few days ago to celebrate your *engagement*, I didn't expect to end the trip by toasting you and your *husband*, James, but I couldn't be more thrilled, and honored, to be doing so tonight. We all know you're the master of nicknames. One I've heard you use many times over the years is 'superstar,' but the truth is *you're* a superstar, Skylar. You're the most successful woman, correct that, *person*, I know, but you're also the most hardworking, the most driven, the most deserving of success. I can't imagine there are many brides out there who conduct not one, but *two* international conference calls on their wedding day! But in addition to killing it professionally, you're also the least pretentious person I know, treating everyone in your path with respect, with compassion, with *warmth*. You excel at everything, but somehow you manage to do it with humility and grace, and without making those not as accomplished as you feel inferior, no matter what some of us may have said in a moment of low self-esteem that had nothing to do with you whatsoever."

Skylar laughed and blew Daphne a kiss.

"Anyhow, I could go on and on about how much I respect you, about how highly I think of you, and how fortunate I am to have you in my life, but tonight I just want to say that I'm so happy for this turn *your* life is taking, that after decades of loving and supporting those around you, you finally found a man—an extremely deserving man—to love and support you back." Daphne looked at James. "And *James*, thank *you* for being that person, for making Skylar happier than I've ever seen her."

"What can I say? I'm a smitten kitten," Skylar said with a shrug.

Krissa nodded. "Yep, you're a smitten kitten,"

Fighting back tears, Daphne took a deep breath and lifted her glass. "I'm going to end this now before I lose it and ruin the makeup that Skylar so generously paid to have applied, so cheers to Skylar and James, and to Sloane too." She made eye contact with Sloane, who gave her a grateful smile in return. "I wish your new family a lifetime of love, laughter … and clear beads."

"To the clear beads!" KC shouted.

Krissa took a gulp of her champagne. "I really should have gone to Northwestern."

# Chapter Thirty-One

"Morning, sweets. You all packed? Coffee's freshly brewed," Skylar pointed to the pot as Daphne took a seat at the kitchen island. Her laptop in front of her, Skylar was dressed in a crisp navy-blue pantsuit with tiny gray pinstripes, her hair pulled back into a sleek low ponytail.

Daphne reached for a mug and poured herself a cup. "All packed and ready to go. You look super stylish, by the way. Like straight out of a catalog. Are you really going to work the day after your wedding?"

Skylar's fingers flew across her keyboard. "Duty calls, unfortunately. I have eleven meetings today."

"*Eleven* meetings? That is insane. I can't say I'm surprised, though. Is James still sleeping?"

Skylar didn't look up from the screen "He left for a breakfast meeting with a client a half hour ago. He said to say goodbye."

Daphne smiled. "You guys are two peas in a pod. Do you think you'll ever find time to go on a proper honeymoon?"

"We'll make time. Probably not for a few months, but don't worry, we'll honeymoon the hell out of somewhere awesome."

"I like that answer." Daphne turned her head toward the hallway. "KC's not up yet?"

"Haven't seen her." Skylar reached for her coffee mug. "I bet she snuck out for a run, that little weasel. She's like an addict."

"I think this *moderation* thing is going to be an adjustment for her," Daphne said.

Just then KC appeared, freshly showered and dressed in street clothes. "I heard that."

"Street clothes, eh? So no run this morning? Or did you sneak out early?" Skylar said.

"My money's on the early sneak out," Daphne said.

"If you must know, I *did* sneak out early, but just for a brisk walk and some light stretching. I figured running every other day is enough for me, at least while I'm pregnant. After the baby comes, it'll be back to balls-out."

"Look at you, being all sensible for the greater good," Daphne said.

"Very maternal of you," Skylar said.

KC pointed to Skylar as she climbed onto a kitchen stool. "You're one to talk about being maternal. Maybe it's the pregnancy hormones, but I cried the other day watching you give Sloane that bracelet."

"Those hormones are having a field day," Daphne said. "You also cried at the wedding, when Skylar and James came home with their marriage license, and at least three other times over the weekend. That's the most I've seen you cry in all the years I've known you—and it all happened in the span of about five days."

"You're right. My tear ducts worked out more this weekend than I did," KC said with a giggle.

Just then Skylar's phone beeped with one text, then another. She picked it up, then burst out laughing.

"What's so funny?" Daphne asked.

"Krissa, God she cracks me up. Check it out." She slid her phone over for KC and Daphne to read the messages.

*Hey Bride, how goes the first day of married bliss? Please give ur besties a goodbye hug 4 me and tell KC I hope she doesn't go through withdrawals from my tragicomical dating stories. So hey just wanted 2 confirm that we're still on for dinner tomorrow so I don't double book. You down for Mexican? I'm craving chicken vaginas.*

*AAAAARGH stupid autocorrect! Chicken FAJITAS hahahaha.*

Daphne and KC both laughed too. "You've got a good one in her," Daphne said.

"Don't I know it." Skylar checked her watch and looked at KC. "You all packed? The car will be here in fifteen minutes."

"Almost, but not quite finished. I am super bummed to be leaving, so I'm dragging my feet a little."

Skylar made a shooing motion at KC. "Well, I hate to see you go, but Max needs you back, not to mention that granddaughter of yours. Now go finish packing, chop chop, remember the flood, and all that jazz."

KC saluted, then turned on her heel and trotted back toward her bedroom.

Daphne read the news on her phone for a few minutes as Skylar continued tapping away at her laptop.

"Done!" Skylar finally said, then stood up to get some more coffee. She refilled her mug, and as she tucked the pot back into the coffee maker Daphne pointed to the computer.

"Can I borrow that for a second? I want to check my e-mail before we leave, and it's so much easier to respond on a keyboard than on my phone."

Skylar slid the laptop across the island. "It's all yours. The password's *3Musketeers*."

"For real?"

Skylar put a finger to her lips. "Don't tell anyone at my office. It's top secret. And a little embarrassing."

"Don't worry, your secret's safe with me." Daphne punched in the password and logged into her account. She scanned her in-box, then blinked when she saw a message from a name she didn't recognize. She clicked to open it, then gasped as she read. She jumped up and pointed to the screen. "Oh my God! Oh my God!"

"Woah, sugar! You okay there? You sound like KC."

"Hey, I heard that!" KC rolled her suitcase into the kitchen.

Daphne kept pointing to the laptop. "Look!"

"If it's that the video of the otter cuddling with a kitten, I've already seen it," KC said.

Daphne shook her head. "No it's … it's an e-mail from an agent. A literary agent. Read it!"

Skylar took a seat in front of the laptop and read out loud. "Dear Daphne, I've just finished your delightful manuscript, *Looking for Lexi*, and while I think it needs work, I believe it has enormous potential and I would love to offer you representation. Please contact me at your earliest convenience to discuss. Cheers, Alex Rach, AR Literary."

Skylar turned to Daphne, who was standing with her mouth agape. "Daphne, this is outstanding!"

Tears began streaming down Daphne's cheeks.

"I thought you said you'd heard from all the agents you'd pitched?" KC said. "Thirty-six, right?"

Tears still flowing, Daphne began to laugh. "I guess it was thirty-five. I told you guys—I'm not great at math."

# Chapter Thirty-Two

That afternoon, Daphne was back in Columbus. Home sweet home. She paid the taxi driver and wheeled her suitcase into her house, a hint of the smile that had attached itself to her face that morning still lingering. Normally Carol would have picked her up at the airport, but she and Norman were vacationing all week in Florida. Daphne would have to wait until Emma got back from Brian's tomorrow to share the good news with a loved one.

In person, that was. She wanted to do it that way to see the look on both Carol's and her daughter's faces. She knew she could do a video call with Emma, but you can't hug your child through a screen, and she was really looking forward to that hug. She also wanted to float the idea of a campus visit to Northwestern, as well as a trip to New York to look at Columbia and NYU. Maybe none of those places would be right for Emma, but maybe they would.

*That's for Emma to decide, and Emma alone.*

After unpacking her clothes and toiletries, Daphne retrieved a hammer and nail from the garage, then pulled out her sketch of the Boathouse and removed the bubble wrap. It was a simple drawing in black and white, but to her it was as vibrant as a kaleidoscope, her imagination filling it not just with color, but with sounds, with smells, with *stories*. She carried it into her office and carefully hung it on the wall, and when she stepped back to see if it was level she felt a rush of memories of her time in New York. She'd been there only a few days, but to her it felt like her whole world had changed.

She looked at the bracelet on her wrist and smiled.

Then she sat down at her desk and began to write.

•　•　•

# Thank You!

If you're a loyal reader of my novels, you probably noticed a larger-than-usual gap between my last release, *Wait for the Rain*, and this one. I didn't plan for that to happen, in fact I hate that it did, but the unfortunate truth is that I spent more than a year working on—forcing, actually—a lackluster story that was going nowhere. In the process I not only lost my joy for writing, but my confidence. When I finally decided to pull the plug on the book, I honestly didn't know if I had it in me to write another one.

Fast-forward a few months, and during a visit home to California I saw my dear friend Annie Flaig, who may be the most kindhearted person I have ever met. Also a devoted fan, she convinced me to get back on the horse, and over dinner we put our heads together and came up with an idea for a story about the power of female friendship. It was a bare-bones outline, but it got me excited to try again, so when I got back to Brooklyn I sat down and started writing. I immediately liked how the plot was unfolding, but I was terrified that I'd lost all perspective, so I sent a few pages to Terri Sharkey, who is my sister Michele's mother-in-law and a big supporter of my work. Terri's brutal-yet-much-appreciated candor regarding my previous effort had proved the integrity of her feedback, so I awaited her response with baited breath. When she said I had my "mojo" back and that she couldn't wait to read more, I exhaled with a huge smile and never looked back. Terri, I will forever be grateful to you for your tough-love honesty.

Once I settled into book-writing mode, as usual I found myself weaving real-life anecdotes and details into the chapters. For those nuggets I have the following friends to thank: Ingrid Bell, Emily Brady, Billy Burkoth, Colleen DeBaise, Annie Flaig, Jamie Tilotta Green, Ariel Hoffman, Courtney Carroll Levinsohn, Niki Marcheggiani, Mitch Miller, Kelly O'Connell, David Pinter, Colleen Roche, Michele Murnane Sharkey, and Adam VanDerven. A special hug goes to my soccer pal Maria Sönnerborg for wearing her Lokai bracelet to a game. Who would have guessed that our conversation that day would lead to this?

After I'd completed the first draft and received an enthusiastic thumbs-up from Tami May McMillan, my buddy and trusted go-to beta reader, I turned the manuscript over to the talented Christina Henry de Tessan, whose developmental editing skills continue to amaze me. I eagerly jumped into the revision phase, and when that was done I hired my highly unpaid proofreader, Flo Murnane, aka Mom, whose red pen got its standard workout. Now it was time to choose a title, which at times seemed more challenging than writing the novel itself. I lost track of how many candidates we discarded before Terri Sharkey came up with *Bridges* and David Pinter suggested adding a subtitle, but many thanks to Lauren Lyons Cole, Mommy Dearest, Annie Flaig, Alison Marquiss, Melissa O'Connell, Peggy Prendergast, Brett Sharkey, Michele Murnane Sharkey, John Scouffas, and Mary Scouffas for stirring the pot of creativity along the way.

So there you have it. I was away, and now I'm back. Here's to the friendships that made it happen!

# About the Author

A former PR executive who abandoned a successful career to pursue a more fulfilling life, Maria Murnane is the bestselling author of *Wait for the Rain, Katwalk,* and International Book Award winner *Cassidy Lane,* as well as the Waverly Bryson series*: Perfect on Paper, It's a Waverly Life, Honey on Your Mind,* and *Chocolate for Two,* which garnered a starred review in *Publishers Weekly.* Originally from California, she now lives in Brooklyn. Learn more at www.mariamurnane.com.

*Photo by Chris Conroy Photography*

Made in the USA
Middletown, DE
26 July 2022

69878093R00158